7/22

S0-BBS-400

BREATHING LIES

(THE CURSE OF HALLOWS HILL, BOOK 1)

JESSICA SORENSEN

Breathing Lies

Jessica Sorensen

All rights reserved.

Copyright © 2018 by Jessica Sorensen

This is a work of fiction. Any resemblance of characters to actual persons, living or dead, is purely coincidental. The author holds exclusive rights to this work. Unauthorized duplication is prohibited. No part of this book can be reproduced in any form or by electronic or mechanical means including information storage and retrieval systems, without the permission in writing from the author. The only exception is by a reviewer who may quote short excerpts in a review. Any trademarks, service marks, product names or names featured are assumed to be the property of their respective owners, and are used only for reference. There is no implied endorsement if we use one of these terms.

ISBN: 9781939045577

For information: jessicasorensen.com

Cover design by MaeIdesign

 Created with Vellum

To Dav, Kiki, and Day, you guys inspire me every day.

PROLOGUE

HARLYNN

W hen I was fifteen, I realized I was in love with my best friend Foster. But I liked him way before that, all the way back in grade school. Back then, though, it was just a crush. Nothing major. My heart was too young to be in love yet. But on my fifteenth birthday there was a single moment when I looked at him and realized.

I was in love with him.

Over the next few years, that love deepened. But I never dared tell him, fearing I'd ruin our friendship, especially if he didn't love me back. Right before we were supposed to be heading to college, though, he said something to me that made me realize it was time to hand him my heart and soul and hope he didn't crush them.

Turns out, all those years of keeping my feelings

locked away was for nothing, because Foster did feel the same way about me. He had for a while. It should've been the perfect moment. And for a split second, it was.

But then everything crumbled.

Shattered.

Just like the life I thought I knew.

Nothing about my life or my world would ever be the same.

But I'm not even sure the life I thought I knew ever really existed.

Maybe it was just an illusion built around me like a grave of lies.

ONE
HARLYNN

SIX YEARS OLD...

I officially have two best friends. Well, maybe they're not my *best* friends, but they're definitely my friends. Since I haven't ever had anyone who I could call friends, I'm really excited. I just hope they'll stay friends with me when school starts. But I'm worried that when we're around other kids, they'll pretend I have cooties, like most of the kids in my neighborhood do. I really hope they don't, though.

"We should dig a hole in the backyard," Foster Avertonson, one of my two new friends, says to me and Kingsley, his twin brother and my other new friend.

Up until about a year ago, I didn't even know they were twins. I always thought twins were supposed to look exactly the same, but Foster and Kingsley don't look anything alike. My mom explained to me that sometimes twins don't always look the same, so I guess it makes sense.

And I'm actually glad they don't look the same, because it'd make it hard to tell them apart. Kingsley has blond hair, and Foster has brown, so it's super easy. Their mom dresses them in the same clothes, though, so that's kind of weird. Right now, they both have on tan pants, light blue shirts, and sneakers. Kingsley told me he hates the clothes his mom picks out, but she makes him wear them anyway. Foster thinks he's crazy, that the outfits are awesome.

"I'm not sure we should," I tell Foster as I tear open a fruit snack.

We're sitting at the kitchen table at my house, which means if we do what Foster wants to do, we'll have to dig the hole in my parents' backyard, and I'll probably be the one to get into trouble.

"Why not?" Foster holds out his hand in my direction, and I dump a few fruit snacks into his palm before offering the rest of my snack to Kingsley.

He shakes his head. "No thanks. I'm not that hungry."

He never takes anything I offer him. I sometimes wonder if he really doesn't like me. That maybe his mom makes him hang out with me when she comes over to have a girls' day with my mom, which basically means they let Kingsley, Foster, and I play while they hang out in the basement, drinking wine and listening to music. I think they might do other things, too, since every time I go down to the basement after one of their girl's day, it smells like a skunk. I asked my dad about it once, and he told me it was my mom's smelly candles. I don't really get why my mom would have a skunk-scented candle, but whatever.

I stuff the rest of the fruit snacks into my mouth then hop off the chair and toss the wrapper into the trashcan. "Maybe we can play a game or something."

"Nah, let's dig a hole in the backyard." Foster gets up, slides the sliding glass door open, and walks outside.

Kingsley heaves a weighted sigh. "I guess we're digging a hole in the backyard."

I frown. "What if we get caught? I'm probably the one who's gonna get in trouble."

He pushes to his feet. "I'll take the fall if we get caught, okay?"

I shake my head. "I don't want you getting in trouble either."

He heads for the door, nodding for me to follow him. "Come on. Even if we don't go out there, Foster's gonna dig the hole anyway."

Still frowning, I follow Kingsley outside and across the backyard to where Foster is waiting for us with a shovel.

"You guys walk as slow as snails," he teases with a grin.

I roll my eyes, smiling back. "Snails don't walk. They slide. And you walk fast. You're like that speedy guy superhero."

Foster lightly tugs on one of my braids. "His name is *The Flash*, silly."

When he pulls his hand away, a few strands of my hair snagged on his watch, and he ends up pulling my head forward. My eyes water.

"Ow." I tip my head down. "My hair's caught on your watch."

My hair gets pulled even harder, and I start to wonder if he's doing it on purpose when he says, "It's not my watch doing it."

I angle my head to the side and frown. It's Kingsley's fingers that are wrapped around my braid.

"Um... why're you pulling my hair?" I ask confusedly.

"I wasn't. I was trying to help you get untangled," Kingsley mutters, letting go of my braid.

"Sure you weren't." Foster glares at his brother. "Why do you have to be so mean all the time?"

I don't think Kingsley is mean, but he does act mad a lot and is always quiet, as if he hates being here—hates me.

Is that why he pulled my hair?

Kingsley scowls at Foster. "Whatever. Can we just dig the stupid hole now?"

Foster hands him the shovel. "Yeah, go ahead."

Kingsley snatches the shovel and gives Foster a dirty look before he starts digging into the ground.

Foster sticks out his hand to me. "Wanna go with me and find some cool stuff to bury?"

Nodding, I take his hand and hike with him toward the trees that line my backyard.

Wait... Is he taking me into the woods?

"Wait," Kingsley calls out. "You guys are seriously going in there?"

Foster waves him off. "We'll be fine."

Kingsley scratches his arm. "Her mom said she's not supposed to go into the woods."

Foster dismisses him with a shrug. "She'll be fine. She's with me."

Kingsley's frown deepens. "I don't think you should go."

Foster rolls his eyes. "Well, it's not your decision, is it?"

Kingsley stares at me as Foster turns to walk away, pulling me with him.

"Don't worry; we'll be fine." Foster gives my hand a squeeze, drawing my attention to him.

Not wanting him to think I'm a scaredy cat, I smile at him. "I know."

He grins then focuses on the path ahead that winds through the trees.

"What sort of stuff are we gonna bury?" I ask, chewing on my fingernail as we step into the shade of the trees.

He shrugs, glancing around before looking down at my neck. He eyes it over. "Hey, what about this?" He points at the locket hanging around my neck. "We could pretend it's buried treasure."

I quickly cover the locket with my hand. "No way. My grandma gave this to me right before she died."

"Oh." He glances at it again then shrugs. "No worries. We can find something else."

I relax, glad he isn't mad at me.

Tugging on my hand, he guides me farther into the forest. We both begin looking for something cool to put in the hole. We walk for so long that my feet start to hurt. I try not to be a baby and keep quiet, but I wish I'd worn a different pair of shoes besides sandals—the insides are starting to fill up with twigs, dirt, and pebbles.

"How much farther are we going to walk?" I ask as I stumble to keep up with Foster's super speedy walk.

He shrugs. "Until I find something awesome to put in that hole."

I don't want to frown, but the odds of finding something cool out here aren't looking very great. Still, I peer around, crossing my fingers I can find something soon—

I trip over something and stumble forward, landing face-first in a bush, branches tangled around me and scraping my palms.

Foster rushes over. "Holy crap! Are you okay?"

I nod, trying to push to my feet, but my hair is snagged. "Can you help me? My hair's stuck on something."

"Yeah, hold still, okay?" He starts unwinding my hair from the branches.

I obey, holding perfectly still. "I don't even know what I tripped over."

"Probably your own feet," he teases. "You're kind of klutzy."

My cheeks warm in embarrassment. "Sorry."

"Don't worry. It's cute. You're really cool, Har."

My cheeks grow even hotter. "Thanks."

He chuckles. "You're welcome."

It takes him a bit, but he manages to get my hair untangled. Then he helps me to my feet.

"Are you okay?" he asks, brushing some twigs out of my hair.

I nod, staring down at my palms. The skin is cut open and blood oozes from the wounds.

"I hurt my hands," I say, showing him.

He traces his fingers along the wounds with a funny look on his face. "We should probably get you home before dirt gets in the cuts. My mom says that sort of stuff causes infections or something. Plus, it looks like a storm's coming."

"Okay." I'm more than grateful we're leaving.

We hurry back up the path toward home, not holding hands this time since mine are all scraped up. The walk back to my house feels longer than when we walked into the forest. The sunlight is slipping away, and the wind is getting chilly. Eventually, we make it out of the trees where it's not nearly so cold or windy, but my hands hurt really bad, so I rush toward my house, glad to be home. My relief quickly turns into fear, though, as I realize my locket isn't bouncing against my neck anymore.

Tears flood my eyes. "Crap."

"What's wrong?" Foster asks, jogging up beside me.

"My locket's gone." I don't want to cry and look like a baby in front of him, but my grandma was one of my favorite people ever, and when she left the necklace to me, it made me feel special.

"Don't cry," Fosters says. "I'll find it."

"No, don't. It's getting too dark ..." I start, but he's already running into the trees.

Frowning, I walk the rest of the distance to my backyard.

"You guys were gone forever," Kingsley mutters as he stops digging.

Just in front of his feet is a large hole, and beside that is a pile of dirt and grass. When my mom sees this, I'll probably be in trouble big time. And since I lost my necklace, too ...

What a bad day.

Tears well in my eyes. "Foster went back into the woods because I lost my favorite necklace, and it's dark, and I'm worried about him, and now there's a hole in the yard ..."

Kingsley sets the shovel down and pats my back. "Don't cry, okay? I'm sure Foster will find your necklace." He glances from the trees to me then to the hole. "As for the hole ... we can hurry up and put all the dirt back in it before anyone sees it."

I wipe the tears from my cheeks with the back of my hand. "But Foster wants to bury something in it."

"Foster will be okay just as long as you stop crying." He offers me a small smile, but it seems stiff, as if he's annoyed or something.

I sniffle. "Are you sure—"

"What in the hell?" My mom storms out of the house

and strides across the grass toward us. Foster and Kingsley's mom is behind her and she looks angry too.

"Shit," Kingsley curses.

My eyes widen at the word. Sure, I've heard my parents use it before, but I've never heard anyone my age say it. It makes Kingsley seem sort of cool and kind of scary.

"Who did this?" my mom demands, her gaze locking on me.

"Um ..." I squirm. "I'm sorry, Mom—"

"It was me." Kingsley steps forward. "It was my idea. Harlynn tried to talk me out of it, but I didn't listen."

"Dammit, Kingsley," his mom scoffs. "Why do you always have to cause trouble?"

Kingsley stares at the ground and mutters, "Do I really need to answer that?"

"No, you really don't." His mom snags ahold of his sleeve. "Come on; you're going home." She scans the backyard, her brows dipping. "Wait. Where's Foster?"

"Right here." Foster appears beside the back fence and jogs up to us with dirt smudged on his face. He takes one look at his mom holding on to Kingsley's sleeve and frowns. "What's going on?"

"Your brother thought it'd be a good idea to ruin the Everly's backyard, even though I warned him before we came over here that if he so much as ruined one single thing, he'd be grounded for a month." She gives Kingsley a dirty look, to which he responds with indifference.

Foster sneaks a glance at his brother then looks back at his mom. "Do I have to go home, too? I was having a lot of fun hanging out with Harlynn." He smiles at me, and I return it, surprised by his words.

With me crying and not wanting to dig a hole, I thought he'd be bored by now.

His mom starts to shake her head, but then she frowns as she glances over at the forest. "Wait. You were in the woods?"

Foster pulls a *whoops* face. "Um, yeah, but I was just looking for Harlynn's locket."

"Why would your locket be in there?" my mom asks me, raising her brows.

Foster's eyes widen as he looks at me and mouths, "*Sorry.*"

"Um ..." I bite on my thumbnail.

My mom's nostrils flare. "All right, everyone inside now."

With our shoulders slumped, Foster, Kingsley, and I trudge toward the house.

"Sorry," Foster whispers to me.

"It's okay," I tell him. "But please tell me you found my locket."

He shakes his head. "But I promise I'll find it. I won't stop looking until I do."

I smile, even though I'm sad my locket is gone. But his offer to look for it is really nice.

"Thanks, Foster." I give him a hug.

When Kingsley frowns at us, I step back and put my arms around him.

"Thanks for taking the fall for the hole," I say, hugging him.

He hugs me back, his arms a little shaky like he's cold, even though the wind has quieted and the air has warmed. Maybe he's like my grandma who used to say her bad circulation made her cold.

He stops shaking as he steps back then quickly hurries inside the house.

I turn toward Foster. "Did I do something wrong?"

"Nah, he just gets weird like that. I'm not sure why, but you probably shouldn't worry about it." He shifts his weight, rubbing the back of his neck. "But maybe you shouldn't hug him again for a while."

I nod and make a mental note not to hug Kingsley again unless he asks me to. Then we go inside.

We get grounded for a month for digging the hole and for wandering into the woods. But we're allowed to hang out with each other, so it's not that bad of a punishment. I think the only reason they allow it, though, is so our moms can still have their girls' day.

We have to fill the hole up, too, but since my hands are messed up, Foster and Kingsley offer to do it. I like them a little bit more for it.

After that, Foster and Kingsley start coming over to my house a lot. Well, Foster does but I don't see Kingsley for about a month. When I ask Foster why, he says its because Kingsley is hanging out with his own friends, which makes me kind of sad. But eventually, Kingsley starts coming over again.

Every time they come to my house, Foster sneaks into the woods to look for my necklace. He never does find it, but I appreciate him trying. That's when I start really liking him.

As for Kingsley, I'm not as close with him as I am with Foster, but we're still friends. That is until my twelfth birthday. That day, I decide it might be better to not be Kingsley's friend anymore.

TWO
HARLYNN
TWELVE YEARS LATER...

I've never thought of myself as one of those sappy, lovey-dovey, get all swoony over a guy sort of girls. Sure, I like guys. I just don't get all gushy and flustered whenever one gives me attention. Take the dude in front of me. His name is Grey, and he's considered one of the most popular guys in Sunnyvale. All through high school, girls were all over him, and he took advantage of it, changing girlfriends about as much as I change hair colors, which I do every few months.

Now that we've graduated, I wonder if Grey will be able to carry his popularity through college. Or will he have peaked in high school? Who really knows? And honestly, I don't care about Grey. He's a douchebag and loves to talk about himself. Just like he is right now.

"Look, I know you don't get it, but could you at least

try to show me some respect? God, Harlynn, do you even realize how many championships I've won? I didn't peak in high school." He takes a sip from the plastic cup he's holding. "I'm a badass. I don't know why you've never understood that."

Yeah, okay, so this conversation might be a little bit my fault.

After Grey cornered me at the bonfire and proceeded to tell me for the umpteenth time how amazing he is, I may have let it slip that perhaps he peaked in high school. It was mostly just to get him to leave me alone. Obviously, it didn't work. I guess I shouldn't be that surprised.

Ever since freshman year after I turned down his invite to go to a dance, he's been trying to get me to go out with him. While I felt bad for rejecting him, there was no way I could've accepted his dance invite. Or, well, his dance *demand*, since he basically walked up to me, put his arm around my shoulders, and said, "Hey, baby, it's your lucky day, because I'm going to take you to the dance." When I politely told him, "No thank you," and slipped out from underneath his arm, he became extremely irritated, but not enough to stop asking me out. He does it every so often when he's between girl-friends. And every single time, I turn him down. I'm not sure why he's so persistent, but I wonder if he secretly gets off on it. I grew tired of it a long time ago and can't wait for college to start since he's going to one clear across the country while I'm going to the local college. That means I'll be far away from him and his need to bug me. Seriously, the guy needs to learn that no means no.

"I don't get you," Grey continues to babble on. "Every girl would love to be in your shoes."

Oh god, here we go again.

I arch a brow. "And why's that?"

He gapes at me. "Because I've asked you out like twenty times!"

"And I've said no to all those twenty times," I remind him then take a sip of my beer. "Newsflash: not every girl wants to date you. And no girl wants to repeatedly have to turn a guy down."

His lips kick up into a smirk, and he reaches out to tuck a strand of hair behind my ear. "Then stop turning me down."

His touch makes my skin crawl.

I start to turn to leave, but he folds his fingers around my arm.

"Hey, I'm sorry. That was probably too pushy, right?"

I give him a blank stare. Is he being serious? Pushy is practically his middle name.

"Yeah, just a bit."

"All right, I'll back off." His gaze drops to the cup in

my hand. "In fact, let me refill your drink as an apology for being so damn annoying."

"No thanks. I'm good."

"Oh, come on. I'm trying to be nice here."

"So am I, but you're not taking the hint." I try to step back, but he tightens his hold on my arm.

I'm about one step away from tossing my drink in his face, not just for hitting on me again but for touching me unwelcomingly, when someone slips an arm around my waist.

Unlike Grey, this touch is welcomed.

Grey immediately releases me.

"Hey," Foster whispers in my ear. "Everything okay?"

I discreetly breathe in his scent; cologne, campfire, and something light and sweet. It reminds me of when we were little and our families would go camping together. Back then, Foster and I were best friends—still are. But around the age of fifteen, I fell in love with him. And not in a best friend sort of way. No, I *love* him, love him. Love spending time with him. Love the way he smells. Love his smile. Love the way he laughs. Love the way his dark hair falls into his eyes ...

Okay, maybe I do get sort of lovey-dovey about guys sometimes, but only on the inside. On the outside, I'm as cool as I always am, which I guess isn't really that cool. Truthfully, I'm sort of awkward and strange.

I love reading and writing more than going out. I'm obsessed with anything that has to do with steampunk, *Alice in Wonderland*, and zombies. I prefer clunky boots over high heels, jeans and T-shirts over dresses, facial piercings over diamond necklaces and, like I mentioned before, love dying my hair all sorts of crazy colors. Right now, it's brown about halfway down—my normal color—but toward the bottom, the strands bleed into various shades of purple and indigo. It's pretty damn badass if I do say so myself, but not everyone is a fan of it. Foster is always telling me that he loves the natural color of my hair and that the crazy colors make me seem wilder than I really am. I've thought about not dying it anymore because of that, but a tiny part of me, a tiny part I rarely admit exists, likes the idea that I look a bit wild.

But I'll never tell anyone that aloud. Especially Foster.

My gaze drifts to Foster as he brushes his fingers through my hair. He's looking at me with concern, but that's nothing new.

He's always worrying about me, because he's my best friend, and because, back when we started high school, our dads gave him a lecture about keeping an eye on me and making sure no one ever hurt me.

Yeah, both our parents are besties, so we were pretty much destined to be best friends. Well, I guess I could say that if it weren't for Kingsley, who I am no longer friends with. Kingsley isn't like Foster, though.

Where Foster is all light, happiness, smiles, and popularity; Kingsley radiates darkness, is a loner, and as far as I know, has only one close friend. And while I feel awful for even thinking it, sometimes Kingsley scares me. I'm not the only one who feels that way. Still, since we were sort of friends when we were younger, I feel bad for feeling the way I do. I have a good reason to, though.

"I'm okay," I tell Foster, hoping to erase some of his worry.

"You sure?" He gives a sidelong glance in Grey's direction then leans toward me and lowers his voice. "Because I can kick some ass if I need to."

A laugh escapes my lips. "As fun as that sounds to watch, I'd like to keep the fights to a minimum, at least for tonight."

He grins wickedly. "Just for tonight?"

"Yeah, remember we have that bar fight scheduled for tomorrow?"

"Aw ... shit, must have slipped my mind. But I'll totally pencil it in, right between packing my stuff and taking you out for ice cream."

My smile falters at the reminder that he'll be leaving for college soon because, unlike me, he decided to start school during summer semester. And since my best friend

Alena is going to be spending the summer in Paris, I'm going to pretty much be spending the summer alone.

"Hey." His smile fades as he reaches up with his free hand and cups my cheek. "I promise I'm going to come back and visit."

"I know, but"—I sigh—"it's like six hours away from here. You're not going to want to make that drive a lot."

He grazes his finger along my cheekbone. "For you, I will."

I roll my eyes. "You're so cheesy sometimes."

"Which is why you love me so much."

God, if only he knew.

Grey clears his throat, startling Foster and me.

"Um, I'm going to get a drink." Grey looks at me. "You sure you don't want me to refill yours?"

"Yep, I already told you I was good."

He frowns, but as his gaze settles on Foster, his lips tug into a smirk. "Hey, man, heard you were taking off to college soon."

Foster drops his hand from my cheek, his lips dipping into a frown. He's never been a fan of Grey. "Yeah, I want to get an early start on things. I'm actually trying to finish my degree in three years instead of four."

Grey's lips twist into a malicious grin. "Huh. That's not the reason I heard you were leaving early."

Foster threads his fingers through mine. "Well, you heard wrong."

Grey's smirk magnifies. "You sure? Because I swear I heard a rumor that you might've told someone you're looking to make a quick escape from Sunnyvale."

I glance at Foster in confusion. "What's he talking about?"

Foster stares Grey down, the afterglow of the fire reflecting in his eyes. "He's just talking out of his ass like he always does."

Grey glares at him. "*I'm* the one who's talking out of my ass? Go fuck yourself. Seriously, you're just as big of a liar as I am." His gaze flicks to me. "You may think I'm a bad guy, and maybe in some ways I am, but so is Foster." At that, he stalks off toward the keg.

"What the hell was that about?" I mutter.

"Who the hell knows?" Shaking his head, Foster focuses on me. "You need to stay away from him, okay? His obsession with you makes me nervous."

This isn't the first time he's said this to me, but the last time it was about someone else. He was right then, though, and probably is now.

"I do try to stay away from him," I insist. "He's the one who won't leave me alone."

"I know, but I ..." He withdraws his arm from around

me and rakes his fingers through his dark hair. "Fuck, I don't know what to do."

He's acting weird and twitchy, so unlike Foster.

"What's going on?" I question. "Wait. Did you get high?"

He frowns. "What? No. Why would you ask that?"

"Because you're freaking out, and you usually only do that when you get stoned."

"I don't every time ... Sometimes, I get relaxed." His gaze travels over my shoulder as he dazes off.

Okay, he has to be stoned. And while I don't mind him occasionally partying it up, Foster sometimes has a bad reaction to getting blazed. Instead of getting super calm, he has mad freak-outs. I've spent a handful of nights talking him down, and I'd rather not do it tonight when it's one of the last nights we get to hang out together before he leaves.

"Come on; let's get you home before you go into complete meltdown mode."

"What?" He blinks a few times, coming out of his daze. Then his lips sink downward. "I already told you I'm not high."

"Then, what's your deal tonight? Because you seem twitchy and ditzy."

"Ditzy?" He grins, pressing his hand to his heart. "I'm not, nor have I ever been, ditzy."

"If you say so," I quip with an eye roll.

He shakes his head, the corners of his lips quirking. "You're asking for it tonight, aren't you?"

I promptly step back, pointing a finger at him. "No way. Don't you even dare."

He cracks his knuckles. "Aw ... now, come on. Deep down, I know you like it when I do it."

"No, I don't. And if you do it, I'll get you back," I warn. "Ten times worse."

"I think I'll take the risk." He lunges at me.

I whirl around to run but only get one step forward before his lean arm envelopes around me. Then, with one swift motion, he scoops me up, flings me over his shoulder, finds the spot right above my knee, my ticklish spot, and digs his fingers in.

"Foster! Don't you even—"

I squeal as he lightly pinches the area.

"Stop!" I cry through my laughter. "Please!"

"Only if you say the magic words," he says as he continues to tickle me.

"Never!" I shout, drawing all sorts of attention.

Smashing my lips together to hold back my laughter, I reach around and pinch his ass.

"Shit." He lets out a string of curses, his muscles winding tightly.

I let out my best evil villain laugh, trying not to take

his aversion to me pinching his ass too personally. "You play dirty, I play dirty. I thought you knew that, bestie?"

"I do." He gently lowers me back to the ground then stares at me with his brows knit.

I grin like the Cheshire cat. "I think the words you're looking for are *Harlynn, you win.*"

"I guess you did." He brushes his fingers along my cheekbone again, and it startles me a little bit.

I mean, sure, he's touched me like this before, but not while staring at me as if he never wants to look away.

What in the hell is going on?

"Are you okay?" I ask.

He nods. "I was just thinking about how sucky it's going to be not having you around all the time."

"Aw, is that your way of saying you're going to miss me?" I play off what he said jokingly, but inside, I'm a bundle of emotions.

I'm going to miss you, too.

"I guess it is." He smiles. "How about we get out of here? We can grab some ice cream or something then go hang out at our spot until the sun comes up."

"That sounds perfect." I force a smile, but my heart squeezes inside my chest.

We've been going up to our spot by the lake for a couple of years now, ever since he got his driver's license. When we do, it's usually after we sneak out of the house or leave a party. We park and talk until the stars go to sleep. Those nights are perfect, and this might be the very last time we get to do it. In fact, I can feel it in my bones, like a warning. An omen.

"Are you okay?" Foster asks worriedly. "You look upset."

"I'm just really going to miss you," I whisper, and then I throw my arms around him.

He hugs me back. "I'm going to miss you, too. More than anyone else in my life."

"That's because I'm awesome," I aim for a joke to avoid bursting into tears.

"You're more than that." The warmth emitting from his eyes makes my lungs tighten. "I love you, Har."

I know he doesn't mean it like how I love him. At least, I don't think he does. But then he starts to lean in ... to kiss me?

Wait. Is he really about to kiss me?

My heart slams against my chest. "I—"

A girl strolls up to us and taps Foster on the shoulder. Our gazes dart to her and we both tense.

No, this isn't just some girl. It's Evalynn.

Shit.

Evalynn is a girl we went to high school with who became infatuated with Foster. She'd follow him around all the time and constantly asked him out. Foster, being the nice guy that he is, always very politely turned her down. One day, though, Evalynn lost it and screamed at Foster in the hallway after he declined one of her date offers. Then she went outside, slashed his car tires, broke all the windows, and wrote *Liar* on the hood of his truck in her blood, which is not only a bit crazy but also made no sense since Foster hardly ever tells lies.

But, anyway, the ordeal with Evalynn happened about six months ago, and we haven't seen or heard from her since. According to rumors around town, she was admitted into a hospital for a while but was released a couple of months ago.

"Hey, I didn't know you were going to be here tonight." Evalynn smiles sweetly at Foster. "I'm so glad you came. I haven't seen you in ages."

Foster squirms, stuffing his hands into his pockets. "Yeah, it has been a while, hasn't it?"

"Too long." She giggles, placing her hand on his chest. "I was thinking maybe we could go somewhere and talk for a bit. Maybe get a bite to eat."

"Um ..." Foster glances at me, his eyes filled with a silent plea.

"Actually, he was about to drive me home so I don't miss curfew," I chime in, and he offers me a grateful smile.

Evalynn cuts her gaze to me. "Can't you drive yourself home?"

"Can't. He's my ride." I shrug. "Sorry."

Her lips spasm, and her eyes darken. "Whatever." A smile takes over her face as she looks back at Foster. "Call me so we can hang out, okay? It can be just like old times." She blows him a kiss, spins around, and skips off toward the fire pit.

People glance in her direction then at Foster and me, question marks filling their eyes.

I shake my head. "That girl is living in Delusional Land, isn't she?"

Foster pinches the brim of his nose. "I wish someone would've warned me she was back in town."

"Maybe no one knew," I offer. "People do look really shocked to see her."

His gaze sweeps the crowd and his frown deepens. "How about we get out of here?"

"Sounds like an awesome idea." I lace my fingers through his and tug him toward the truck, but then pause. "Wait. Are you sober?"

He chuckles, his sullen mood fading. "Of course. I'd never even suggest getting behind the wheel if I wasn't, especially with you as a passenger."

"Such a good boy." I pat his head like a dog. "Maybe, if you're extra good, I'll give you a special treat tonight."

He sucks his bottom lip between his teeth. "What sort of treat are you offering? Because you say stuff like that and my mind instantly goes to you and lap dances and lacey underwear."

My cheeks erupt with heat and I swat his arm. "You're such a perv."

"Hey, you're the one who offered me a special treat."

"I meant like a back rub or something."

A haughty grin pulls at his lips. "You can do that in your underwear, too. It doesn't have to be a lap dance."

My face is on fire. Luckily, the sky is kissed with only stars and moonlight, so the darkness hides my embarrassment.

I'm acting ridiculous. I know that. And it's not like he's never teased me like this. But, since I've often dreamt about giving Foster a lap dance in my underwear, it's difficult not to get flustered.

"You're adorable when you blush," he whispers in my ear. Then he drapes his arm around me and kisses my cheek. "Come on; let's head up to the lake so we can have a few hours alone together before sunrise. Plus, I'd really rather not be here while Evalynn's around."

I nod, and then we head to his truck with the wind gusting around us, a feeling of agony and loss seeping into me. As if something bad is about to happen.

THREE
HARLYNN

After Foster and I ditch the party, I try to shove the bad feeling I have aside and focus on having fun. On our way to the lake, we make a stop at the one and only gas station in town that's open this late to get something to eat.

"Let's go feed you before you turn into a little gremlin," Foster teases as he hops out of the truck.

Nodding, I get out and meet him around the front. Then we start across the parking lot just as a beat-up GTO pulls in.

"Is that Kingsley?" I'm not sure why I even ask. We live in a really small town where practically no one has the same car.

Foster tracks my gaze and his expression plummets. "Fuck, what's he doing here?"

His reaction is normal—Foster is never happy to see his twin brother.

"Well, it is a public gas station," I tease, nudging him with my elbow.

"I know, but ..." He shakes his head as he yanks open the door to the gas station, a dinging bell announcing our entrance. "I'm just not in the mood to see him." He holds the door open, gesturing for me to go in first.

"You're never in the mood to see him," I remind him as I walk inside.

"Yeah, and for good reasons," he mumbles, letting the door swing shut behind us. Sighing, he wanders toward an aisle, his frown deepening with each step.

So much for one of our last nights together not being ruined. But Foster's relationship with his brother is complicated. When they were younger, the two of them fought a lot until Kingsley finally began ignoring Foster. Foster hasn't been able to stand Kingsley since that happened, and now whenever the two of them are near each other, tension flows through the air.

Sighing at the idea that may happen tonight, I start after Foster.

But as I pass by the window, my gaze drifts to the parking lot just outside where Kingsley's GTO is parked near the side of the building, in the farthest and darkest corner. The headlights are off, and he's leaning against the car. Dressed head to toe in black, he nearly blends in with the night, except for his blond hair, which looks pale in the moonlight. He's not alone either. His friend Porter is standing by the car with his hands tucked in his pockets, his gaze shifty, making me question what they're up to.

Foster has a theory that they started dealing and doing drugs and told me I need to make sure to stay away from them. He could be right, but I don't know. Kingsley doesn't look like a drug addict.

Forcing my thoughts away from Kingsley, I head to find Foster, crossing my fingers that Kingsley will leave by the time we return to Foster's truck. If not and Foster has to cross paths with his brother, his mood is going to nosedive.

Worry plagues my mind as I make my way back to the soda fountain, where Foster is filling up an extra-large cup. As I get nearer, I notice he's chatting with a pretty girl wearing a flowery black dress. She's twirling a strand of her long, brown hair around her finger as she smiles at him. I can't remember her name, but she was a junior when we were freshmen, and while I never saw Foster hang out with her, with how chatty the two of them are, I wonder if they know each other.

I stop in the closest aisle, debating whether or not to join the conversation. When Foster flashes her a flirty smile, I decide to walk away.

I hate that I react this way and know I have no right to. We're not together. Never have been. And he's never shown any signs of wanting to be. But my heart is stupid, I guess.

"When are you going to realize he's never going to see you as more than a friend?" someone asks from beside me.

My gaze snaps up to the side and meets the brown eyes belonging to Porter.

With short, dark hair, even darker eyes, black clothes, and facial piercings and tattoos, most people look at Porter and think gorgeous *bad boy*. But I knew Porter back when he was a scrawny elementary schooler who wore glasses and clothes a size too small for him. Around freshman year, though, he had a growth spurt, put on some weight, and reinvented himself into the beautiful swan he is today. Well, that is, if swans had tattoos, piercings, and a foul mouth.

His reinvention happened about the same time he became friends with Kingsley, who'd already settled into his bad boy status. I think their piercings and tattoos obsessions were the basis of their friendship, but who the hell knows? What I do know is that, the more time they hang out, the more their metal and ink collections multiply. Not that I think it's awful. In fact, I have a couple of piercings myself, including one in my lip that I got for my eighteenth birthday. It was probably the craziest thing I've ever done. I'd actually wanted to do it sooner, had thought about it for a couple of years, but I knew my parents wouldn't approve, which they didn't. Just like I knew Foster wouldn't like it either, which he didn't.

"Why would you do that?" he'd asked after he first noticed the glint of metal ornamenting my lip. "Your lips were so pretty."

"So they're not pretty now?" I'd joked. Or well, tried to joke, but truthfully, I was kind of annoyed, even if he did say my lips were pretty.

"No, they still are but..." He shrugged. "I'm just not a fan of piercings."

And I'm not a fan of football and game night parties, yet I go to stuff like that to support you, I wanted to say back, but I bit my tongue and settled on, "Well I like it."

He'd looked at me like I was crazy. "It just seems weird. I mean, I've never heard you mention you wanted to pierce your lip and then suddenly you do."

"I've thought about doing it before," I admitted. "I just never brought it up because I know you don't like piercings."

He mulled over something, an accusing look rising on his face. "You know, Kingsley has a lot of piercings."

I frowned. Not because Kingsley has a lot of piercings, but because Foster pointing out that I'd done something like Kingsley was an insult. Not that I was certain he meant it that way, but with how much Foster despised Kingsley, it was the only way I could take it.

I almost took the piercing out, but a couple of minutes later, Foster had started flirting with some girl and I decided to leave the piercing in because what did it matter if I took it out? Whether my lips were metal-free or not, Foster was never going to see me as someone he wanted to date.

I blink back to reality as Porter smirks at me. "Are you zoning out on me or just stunned by my good looks?"

"Leave me alone. I'm so not in the mood for your asshole remarks tonight." I swing around him and veer down the candy aisle, giving a discreet glance around to see if Kingsley wandered in with Porter, but I don't spot him anywhere.

"Hey, I'm not an asshole and my remarks aren't either." Porter follows me, being his chatty self, unlike Kingsley, who rarely talks to anyone.

"If you say so." I stop in the candy section and eye over the selection.

He stops beside me and crosses his arms. "I don't know why you're so mean to me. I'm always nice to you."

I arch a brow at him. "Every single time you talk to me, you insult me."

He rubs his scruffy jawline. "How did I insult you just barely?"

"You didn't," I lie, because saying the truth aloud would mean admitting I want Foster to see me as more than a friend.

"Then, why did you just say I did?"

"I never said you insulted me now. Just that you usually do."

He smirks. "No, you said *always*."

I roll my eyes. "Go away and leave me alone, dude."

"Why? So you can go back to watching Foster flirt with that chick over there?" he asks, snatching up a bag of Skittles.

I feel too exposed. "That wasn't what I was doing."

"Yeah, you were." He tears open the bag and pops a few pieces into his mouth. "FYI, you're like ten times hotter than Beth Trelarallie. And a hell of a lot smarter."

I roll my eyes, but then frown in confusion. "Who the hell is Beth?"

"Your lover boy's current conquest." He glances at Foster and the girl— Beth Trelarallie. "Poor girl. I should probably go warn her that the guy she's talking to is a total player who likes to fuck with girls' minds."

"Oh, shut up. I'm so tired of you talking badly about Foster just because Kingsley doesn't like him." I steal the opened bag of candy from him, pour a handful into my palm, then return it to him. "And thanks for buying me a snack." I pop the candy into my mouth and grin.

"Joke's on you since I'm not paying for that, so technically, you just aided in shoplifting." He dumps the rest of the candy into his mouth, tosses the empty bag onto a shelf, then flashes me a cocky grin.

I swallow down the mouthful of candy. "Maybe I'll buy the bag myself."

His brow curves upward. "Are you going to?"

No. "Sure."

"Liar." His grin is all sorts of amused wickedness as he leans in. "Face it, you can pretend to be a good girl, but deep down, we both know you're a little bad." He gives me a knowing look.

I internally grimace. I hate that he knows a secret of mine, about a night when I ditched Foster and pretended to be a different person. Where I hung out with people I didn't know and did stuff I normally wouldn't do.

"Just because I rebelled one time doesn't mean I'm bad," I say, but I feel like such a liar.

That night, when I pretended to be a different person, I felt more like myself than I ever had. But that girl I was that night scared me. Because she doesn't fit into the world I've lived in for over a decade now.

"It may have only been one night, but I'd never seen you look more alive than when you were at that party."

"You're so weird."

"And you're a liar," he says. "We both know that

this"—he points at me then at Foster—"isn't who you really are." He crosses his arms and stares me down. "Personally, I think you ended up with the wrong Avertonson brother, and I think, deep down, you know that." A smile curls at his lips. "You could always let your real self out for a night and come hang out with us tonight."

"No thanks. I still have my fill from the last time we hung out." I smile sweetly at him. "And honestly, that night is one of my biggest regrets." I'm such a liar and he probably knows it.

I hate that he does.

His lips kick up into a smirk. "Even what happened in the closet?"

That remark strikes a nerve.

"You know what? I'm done chatting. I've got candy to pay for." I pick up the empty bag of candy from off the shelf and spin around toward the register.

Really, I have no intention of paying for it. This is all for show and to prove a point that I'm not bad and that I didn't end up with the wrong Avertonson brother. The truth, though, is that sometimes I wonder if I did. If maybe Foster is too good for me.

As I start up the aisle, I throw a smirk over my shoulder at Porter. He mirrors my smirk then winks at me. Confusion sets in. A second later, I walk straight into something hard and solid and that smells familiar, like cologne with a hint of smoke.

I know that scent ...

I stumble back. "Sorry," I apologize to Kingsley, taking another step back as my heart races. "I didn't see you ... I was smirking at Porter instead of paying attention to where I was going." I put on a smile despite being frazzled.

Kingsley always makes me feel this way. He makes a lot of people feel this way. But, while most people's reactions are based on his rough appearance or the rumors around town, mine stems from a few very defining and intense moments that happened between Kingsley and me.

His gaze travels to Porter then zeroes in on me again. "Why were you smirking at him?" he asks curiously.

"Um, because he's annoying." I grin, but inside I feel a bit shaky being so close to him. "Since you're his best friend, I figured you already knew that."

His lips quirk, the slightest trace of a smile materializing. A rare occurrence for him, and I'll admit, he looks beautiful.

Okay, if I'm being truly honest, Kingsley is gorgeous but in a completely different way than Foster. Where Foster has short, styled hair, metal and ink-free skin, a muscular build, and dresses more preppily; Kingsley's blond hair is grown out to his chin, his skin is a work of art, his build is leaner, and almost every drop of clothing he wears is either grey or black and has tears or studs on it. Both of them are tall, but that's about where their common traits stop. Well, except for the same full lips and blue eyes. They both have those. And while I don't like admitting it to myself, sometimes in the deepest darkest part of me—probably the same part that convinced me to go to that party that night without Foster—I feel attracted to Kingsley in a way that I'm not comfortable with. Because I shouldn't be attracted to Kingsley. Not after the stuff he's done to me, yet I am. And it makes me feel beyond confused every single time I'm around him.

"Yeah, maybe." His smile fizzles as his gaze darts to my right. "Although, *he* can be a lot worse."

I track his gaze, a frown forming at my lips. "Foster's not annoying." I sigh, returning my attention to Kingsley, only to find him staring at me intensely. The moment our gazes collide, though, his expression turns blank. But that's typical Kingsley MO—rarely showing any other emotion besides indifference.

"Look, I know you don't owe me anything, but I'm begging you." I clasp my hands in front of me for dramatic effect. "Please don't start a fight with Foster tonight. It's probably going to be one of the last times we get to spend together before you guys leave for college, and all I want is to get out of this gas station and up to the lake without any drama."

His gaze sears into mine. "I never start fights with him."

I resist a sigh. "That's not true."

"Yes, it is," he insists.

This time, a sigh does slip from my lips. "I've witnessed hundreds of fights between you guys. And I get that you don't fight as much as you did when you were kids, but you still do sometimes."

"Those aren't fights," he says, shifting his weight.

"Then, what are they? Arguments? Because, in my opinion, those are one and the same."

He rubs his hand across his face. "You know what? Forget I said anything." He moves to step around me, but I wrap my fingers around his arm, stopping him.

"Please don't start a fight with him," I utter softly.

A shaky breath falters from his lips as his gaze drops to where my fingers are wrapped around his arm. "I won't," he utters, lifting his gaze to mine.

My breath gets ripped from my chest. So much worry and pain flows from his eyes that he's nearly unrecognizable. Kingsley, the epitome of indifference, looks as though he's scared out of his damn mind.

Why? What could be scaring this seemingly cold and unfeeling guy?

I swallow shakily. "Are you okay?"

"Are... you?" He sounds as breathless as I feel, his gaze straying from my hand on his arm to my eyes. Question marks flood his eyes.

I nod. "Yeah ... I'm just worried about you ... You look upset."

"You're worried about me?" He stares into my eyes with his brows knit, then with an uneven breath, he reaches out and tucks a strand of hair behind my ear. "I'm fine. I just wish—"

"What're you doing?" Foster appears beside us with a drink and a tub of ice cream in his hands. His gaze shifts between me and Kingsley, and then to my hand on Kingsley's arm. His jaw works from side to side as he looks at me. "Is everything okay?"

Kingsley's little hair tucking move has me feeling off balance inside. He rarely touches me, hasn't since we were kids after he gave me my first kiss. We were ten and it was on the cheek, so technically, it wasn't a real kiss. But I still count it as one. Maybe I shouldn't. Alena says I shouldn't. That Kingsley is weird and trouble, and I should forget about the time he brushed his lips across my cheek to try to make me feel better after my pet fish died. But it was a good moment, back before all the shittiness between us happened, and I sort of want to latch on to it.

Latch on to the memory of who Kingsley used to be. Or who I thought he used to be.

I lower my hand from Kingsley's arm and, as casually as I can, manage a shrug despite my erratic heartbeat. "Everything's fine," I tell Foster. "We were just talking."

When Foster cocks a brow at me, seeming a bit peeved. I shrug again, unsure what else he wants me to say.

Kingsley and I may not get along, but that doesn't mean I'm some terrible person if I talk to him when we *literally* run into each other. And we wouldn't have even bumped into each other if Foster hadn't been so busy flirting with Beth.

"Stop looking at me like that. It's not that weird," I say to Foster, and Kingsley gives me a questioning look.

Clearly he thinks it's weird. And I guess it sort of is. But again, I *literally* ran into him.

Foster narrows his gaze on his brother. "Why are you even here?"

Kingsley scrubs his hand over his head as he stares down at the floor. "It's a gas station, man."

Foster grinds his teeth. "Everywhere you go, you cause problems. So, do Har and me a favor and stay the hell away from us." He snatches ahold of my hand. "The last thing I need is you ruining our night." He tugs on my arm as he strides away from Kingsley, reacting just how I expected.

It's the reason I begged Kingsley not to start a fight with him.

Kingsley held true to his word too. It's Foster who caused the drama.

Wiggling my hand from his, I slam to a halt.

Foster skids to a stop as well, turning to face me with a crease forming between his brows.

"What's wrong?" he asks, setting the drink and the tub of ice cream on the counter by the register.

I hate confronting him about stuff that I know is going to irritate him, but this is really bothering me. "Why did you do that?"

He digs his wallet out of his pocket as the cashier rings up his stuff. "Do what?"

I cross my arms. "Get pissed off at Kingsley? He didn't do anything."

He slaps a ten-dollar bill on the counter. "He didn't do anything? He was hitting on you.'"

I gape at him. "Are you high tonight? I mean, I was mostly joking earlier, but now I'm wondering if you really are."

He glares at me while the cashier, a thirty-something-year-old dude with an overly large mole on his cheek, raises his brows at us.

I roll my eyes at him. "Don't look at me like that. It's legal here." *If you're twenty-one.* But I don't bother pointing that out.

He lifts his hands in front of him. "Whatever." Then he places Foster's change onto the counter.

Foster picks up the change and stuffs it into his pocket. He doesn't utter another word as he collects his drink and the ice cream, threads his fingers through mine, and pulls me along with him. Part of me wants to pull away, but the other part of me—the part controlled by my stupid heart—won't allow me to.

As we walk silently across the parking lot, holding hands, the stillness between us is uncomfortable. And it only gets worse when we climb into his truck and he starts up the engine, still not uttering a damn word.

I feel like I should say something—crack the tension— but I'm not even positive what's causing it. Because I was talking to Kingsley? Because he thought Kingsley was flirting with me?

I sweep a strand of hair behind my ear, just like Kingsley did to me right before Foster walked up to us. Is that what this is about? Because Kingsley touched my hair? If so, that's stupid. It didn't mean anything, nor did I ask Kingsley to do it.

"I got these for you," Foster mumbles, handing me the drink and the tub of ice cream.

"Thanks." I set the ice cream down and take a gulp of the soda. Dr. Pepper. My favorite.

He nods then plunges back into silence as he straps on his seatbelt. When he moves to put the shifter into drive, he suddenly withdraws his hand and grips the steering wheel.

"Fuuuck," he grits out with his head lowered. "Why does my brother always have to ruin everything?"

I set the drink into the cupholder. "I don't want to piss you off more, but I don't think he was the one who ruined things this time."

He flexes his fingers then lifts his head. "I'm sorry for freaking out on you in there."

"You didn't freak out on me. But you did freak me out with all that Kingsley-flirting-with-me talk." I twist in the seat to face him. "I don't know why you'd say that. It's not true."

His brow meticulously arches, but his lips remain sealed.

"He wasn't flirting with me." I huff out an exasperated breath. "Kingsley doesn't flirt with anyone."

"He doesn't a lot, but sometimes he does." He pauses. "With you. He just doesn't do it in an obvious way."

"You know what? I think I should drive, because I'm officially convinced you're high." I reach over to snatch the keys from the ignition, but he captures my fingers.

"Please stop saying that." Instead of letting my hand go, he traces the folds between my fingers. "Stop thinking I'd ever drive around high, especially with you in the car."

My body wants to shiver so damn badly from his touch, but I refuse to let it. "All right, I'll stop saying it, just as long as you stop saying Kingsley was flirting with me."

"He was, though," he utters. Then he gives me an innocent smile. "That was the last time, I swear."

I stick out my free hand with my pinkie hitched. "Pinkie swear?"

He hitches his pinkie with mine. "I pinkie swear on my life."

I smile at that. "You're so overdramatic sometimes."

He tightens his pinkie on mine when I start to pull away. "I'm only overdramatic about the things that matter."

My heart flutters, but I tell it to calm the hell down, that he's just goofing around.

"You must really think spiders matter then." I press my lips together, stifling a laugh.

"Just because I want to leave the room when I see a spider, doesn't mean I'm being overdramatic," he says, scowling playfully at me.

"*Want* to leave the room? Try more like run out squealing like a Banshee."

He narrows his eyes, but it's another playful move. "I'm a guy. I never squeal."

"Oh, guys can squeal, even louder than girls. That whole term 'squeal like a little girl' is bullshit."

"Yeah, maybe." He stares at me for a heartbeat longer then draws my hand toward his mouth by the pinkie and places a soft kiss against my knuckles. "I'm sorry I started a fight tonight. I just don't like my brother hitting on you. All he does is get in trouble, and I don't want him bringing his shit into your life."

"He won't," I promise. When doubt fills his expression, I stress, "Even if he was hitting on me, it's not like I hit on him back. I don't think of Kingsley like that."

What a liar I am. It makes me feel weird inside. Twisted. I mean, how can I be in love with Foster yet be attracted to his brother? And a brother he despises? It feels like I'm secretly betraying Foster for just having lustful thoughts about Kingsley.

But I can't help it. I swear sometimes I'm like two people. The girl I am when I'm around Foster and the girl who snuck off to a party and kissed a random stranger.

"Good." A smile touches Foster's face, but then it vanishes as he pats his pockets. "Shit, I think I left my wallet on the counter."

"Okay, you're definitely ditzy sometimes," I tease, glad we're no longer fighting.

He winks at me. "That's because you always have me distracted, baby."

I pretend to dry heave, and he chuckles before hopping out of the truck and jogging into the gas station.

I start to relax back in the seat when Porter strolls out of the gas station. He doesn't glance in my direction as he crosses the parking lot and approaches a car with tinted windows parked beside Kingsley's GTO.

Smoke snakes out from the open window as Porter approaches the driver's side door and lowers his head and hand into the cab. The exchange is brief, and then Porter lazily jogs over to Kingsley's car and hops in on the passenger side.

I'm not sure what the hell just happened, other than maybe he just bought drugs. If Foster were here and saw that, he'd blame it on drugs. He does that a lot.

When we were about fourteen, he even tried to convince me that Kingsley and Porter were going to turn into drug dealers and addicts.

"He just seems like the type," he says as he picks handfuls of grass. We are sitting on the front lawn of the middle school, eating our lunch underneath our favorite tree.

"What makes a person the type to do drugs?" I ask, picking the crust off my sandwich.

He shrugs, stealing a chip from my bag. "The kind who gets in trouble and who likes darkness."

"That's a weird way to describe it," I tell him, and Foster shrugs again. I sigh. "And we get in trouble sometimes," I remind him then take a bite out of my sandwich.

"Yeah, but we don't like to get in trouble." He pops the chip into his mouth.

I'm not so sure I agree with him. Sometimes I like getting in trouble. Nothing too bad, of course. But just enough to get my heart racing. I don't believe, though, that the desire will turn me into a drug addict. And Foster saying so makes him sound like he's stereotyping. But I don't say any of this aloud. I learned a long time ago that, when it comes to Foster talking about Kingsley, it's best to say less and let the conversation end quickly.

And a moment later, it does as Foster gets preoccupied with a girl wearing a short skirt and way too much lipstick, something that's starting to happen more frequently ...

The memory gets cut off as Kingsley jogs out of the gas station, his gaze zeroing in on Foster's truck. He stares at it, appearing torn as he stuffs his hands into his pockets. I could roll down the window and see if he needs something—and part of me wants to—but I don't want to risk starting another fight with Foster, so I leave the window up.

Pressing his lips together, Kingsley yanks his attention off me and hurries over to his car. Instead of getting in, he chucks his keys to Porter then jogs over to the car with the tinted windows. He basically does a repeat of what Porter did, leaning down and sticking his hand inside the window. Then he steps back and into the moonlight. He'd be the portrait of beauty if I wasn't fairly sure he might've just bought drugs.

My heart tightens in my chest, begging me to help him, but how? And do I dare after what happened all those years ago?

After he lowers his head, he gives a quick glance at Foster's truck then hops into his car. The car with the tinted windows peels out of the parking lot, but the GTO remains there, leaving me to wonder what they're doing.

Leaving me to wonder just how far into the darkness Kingsley has gone.

Leaving me to wonder a lot of things.

FOUR
HARLYNN

I sit in the car for ten minutes before texting Foster to see what's taking him so long. Then I notice his phone is on the dash, so I hop out of the truck and head inside to find him.

When I enter the gas station, I find him back by the soda machines, staring at the floor.

"I can't find my wallet anywhere," he says with a pout as I approach him. "I thought I left it at the register, but I didn't see it there."

"That's the last place I remember you having it." I stuff my hands into my back pockets, wondering if I should tell him what I just witnessed occur in the parking lot. Then again, maybe Foster isn't the best person to talk to about this. Perhaps I should talk to Kingsley first before I send a pissed-off Foster after him. But, do I even want to get involved in Kingsley's problems? A handful of years ago, I'd have said yes. Now, though ... *so much has happened between us.* "You took it out when you paid."

His forehead creases. "I checked up there already and didn't see it."

"Did you ask the cashier if he has it?"

He snaps his fingers and points at me. "Smart thinking."

I roll my eyes. "So ditzy."

He grins then saunters off toward the register, with me following after him. But I slow to a stop as I pass the snack aisle and spot Beth staring aimlessly at the selection of chips.

Jesus, what does this girl do? Just hang out at the gas station all day? Then again, I guess we've been here as long as she has.

As if sensing me staring at her, she glances over at me. I give a smile and a little wave, even though I don't like her. But my dislike is based entirely on stupid reasons that aren't her fault.

She smiles tightly in return then wraps her arms around herself and goes back to staring at the chips. She doesn't reach for a bag, simply stares, tears welling in her eyes.

I start to ask her if she's okay when someone tugs on

the hem of my shirt. When I twist around, Foster is standing behind me.

"You okay?" he asks with his brows knit.

"Yeah ... But that girl you were talking to earlier seems upset ..." I trail off as Beth rushes past us, choking on a sob. "Bye, Foster."

He sighs then tows me toward the counter. "She just found out her dog died," he explains.

"Poor girl." Despite the fact that she was hitting on Foster earlier, I feel bad for her.

Besides, it's not like she knows about my crush on Foster. And even if she did, Foster and I aren't together, so she has every right to hit on him.

Foster smiles at me like I'm the cutest thing in the world then tucks a strand of hair behind my ear, just like Kingsley did earlier.

"So adorable," he mumbles, causing my cheeks to warm. Grinning, he faces the counter and asks the cashier, "Hey, man, have you seen a wallet?"

The cashier scowls as he reaches around to the side of the register, picks up a wallet, and slaps it down on the counter.

"Thanks," Foster tells him, stuffing his wallet into his back pocket.

The cashier scowls at him. "Whatever."

Foster sighs and steers me toward the door with him.

"What a weirdo," I utter under my breath after we've walked outside.

"Definitely." Foster skims his thumb along the back of my hand. "How about we get out of here before we run into any more distractions?"

"Sounds good to me." I walk with him toward his truck, more than ready to get out of here before any more potential night-ruining forces creep up on us.

WHEN WE PULL out of the gas station, Kingsley's car hasn't moved from the parking spot and a trail of smoke is now snaking out of the cracked open windows. Great. Either he's smoking cigarettes or something else.

I internally sigh as we pull onto the road right as the GTO vacates the parking lot. But it drives in the opposite direction than we're heading, putting the chance of us crossing paths with Kingsley very low.

As we drive toward the lake, Foster is acting like his joking, normal self but seems a bit distracted. My bet is he's still wound up about Kingsley, but I don't ask, wanting to keep the rest of the night as upbeat as possible.

I'm about to crank up some tunes when my phone buzzes from inside my pocket. Noting the time, I assume it's my mom, but the message is from Alena.

Alena: Hey! Are you still at the party? I can't see you anywhere.

Me: Nah, I took off about an hour ago. Sorry I didn't tell you, but you seemed kind of distracted with Jay. Or, well, your lips did.

Alena: You saw that, huh?

Me: Of course I saw! You guys were standing right by the fire! Everyone probably saw.

Alena: Yeah, I guess we weren't very discreet, were we?

Me: Were you trying to be?

Alena: No. Well, maybe. Idk ...

Me: All right, what's up?

Alena: It's nothing. I just think Jay might only want to hook up, which I'm totally fine with ... I think. But I really didn't want anyone knowing about it.

Poor Alena. She's been in love with Jay since freshman year, but he's only recently started paying attention to her. I'm not sure why. Alena is gorgeous. All dark, flowing hair and curves. But she's also very strong and smart and speaks her mind, and Jay has always seemed attracted to girls who don't have much interest in anything but hooking up. Not that I have anything against those girls. To each their own. But Alena isn't like that, which is why I was a bit shocked when I saw her making out with Jay in public without even going on a date with him first.

Me: Lena, I love you to death, so please don't take this the wrong way, but I'm not sure if you should hook up with Jay.

Alena: It's fine. I mean, I think I want to.

Me: The fact that you keep typing "I think" should tell you everything you need to know.

Alena: Yeah, I know. It just really bums me out because I don't think he wants to do anything else. I've liked him forever and it's just so … disappointing.

Me: Maybe that's a sign it's time to move on from Jay. In my opinion you deserve someone way better. And smarter. And who doesn't see winning a burping contest as an achievement.

Alena: He's so hot, though.

Me: There're a lot of other hot guys in Sunnyvale.

Alena: Hmmm … Are you sitting by one of them right now?

My gaze strays to Foster.

"Is that your mom?" he asks, shifting gears.

I shake my head. "It's Alena."

He returns his hand to the steering wheel. "Did she hook up with Jay tonight?"

"Nope, I think we caught most of their show."

"Good. Jay's kind of an asshole."

I eye him warily. "I thought you guys were sort of friends?"

He shrugs. "We used to be until I realized he's an asshole."

"Did something happen?" I ask as a text message pings through.

Alena: If you don't answer, I'm going to assume you two are hooking up right now.

"Not really. He's just always running his mouth about dumb shit, and I got tired of it." His tone is filled with indifference, but his shoulders are rippling with tension. Before I can press him for more details, he leans over the console to glance at my phone. "So, what's Alena saying?"

I hurriedly press my phone to my chest. "That's none of your business."

A smile plays at his lips. "You're awfully squirmy. Makes me really curious what you guys are texting about."

I shrug then take a sip of my soda. "All the hot guys we've made out with."

Curiosity sparkles in his eyes. "Together?"

I swat his arm. "Don't be gross."

"You and Alena kissing ..." he says through a chuckle. "Yeah, that's not gross."

"I never said it was just Alena and me kissing," I quip. "I said it was Alena and me and hot guys kissing."

He chews on his bottom lip, studying me with amusement. "When do I get my turn?"

"Oh, good god," I groan, letting my head bob back against the headrest.

He chuckles, giving my knee a squeeze. "Relax, I'm just messing with you." He skims his finger along the inside of my knee, and goosebumps sprout across my flesh. "I know you, Har. And I know you've never made out with anyone."

Actually, that's not true. I made out with a guy once, but I never told anyone about it. Not even Alena. Why? Well, mostly because I have no clue who I kissed, which sounds weird, but it's the truth. It happened one night while I was at a party. The party Porter mentioned earlier. A party that Foster would flip out about if he knew I went, which is kind of why I did it. I was so sick and tired of going to parties with him and watching him flirt with girl after girl.

"Wait. Has that changed?" Foster suddenly asks.

I shake my head, not ready to divulge the night I made out with a total stranger because of some silly game. "Nah, I'm still a virgin kisser."

When he visibly relaxes, I question why.

I may have grown a pair of lady balls and asked him, but another message from Alena comes through and distracts me.

Alena: You're with Foster, right? And you're planning on being with him all night?

Me: Yeah, I'm with him. Not sure how long we're going to be out, though.

Alena: But you're not wandering off by yourself? Or coming back to the party?

Me: Wasn't planning on it. Why? What's up?

Alena: I think some girl's drink was drugged. One of her friends noticed something was off before she wandered off alone.

Holy shit ...

Me: Did they take her to the hospital?

Alena: I think so.

Me: If they haven't, you need to tell them to take her.

Alena: I'll keep an eye out for them, but I'm pretty sure they did.

Me: Please tell me you're leaving the party.

Alena: Yep, about to head out to my car now.

Me: Don't drive if you've been drinking, especially if drinks are being drugged.

Alena: I didn't drink tonight. My mouth was too preoccupied by something else.

Me: Lol, you're so funny. But seriously, be careful, okay? Have someone walk you to your car.

Alena: Asking Jay right now. You stay safe, too. In fact, I'm going to text Foster and tell him to keep an extra close eye on you tonight. ;)

Me: Please don't.

Alena: ;)

I groan. Good god, I love her to death, but that girl seriously drives me crazy sometimes.

"Everything okay?" Foster asks.

I shove my phone into my pocket. "Alena just texted me again and said some girl's drink was drugged at the party."

His eyes widen. "Holy shit. For reals?"

I nod. "It's crazy. I mean, Alena says the girl's okay and everything, but still, it's scary."

"Definitely scary." He nods in agreement. "I'm glad we left."

"Me, too," I agree, wrapping my arms around myself as a shiver breaks out across my skin.

I'm not even positive why I'm freaking out so much. I've heard of stories like this before. I know this sort of stuff happens. My mom's given me at least ten lectures about never leaving my drinks unattended and only drinking what I pour myself. Still, it's unnerving that there are people out there who do this sort of stuff. Who want to take advantage of people. Who want to shatter people.

Evil, that's what they are. That's all there is to it. And tonight, I may have looked at them, saw them unknowingly.

I shiver. Tonight, I might have seen evil.

FIVE
HARLYNN

After I inform Foster about the girl's drink getting drugged, he pulls over to send a text to some of his friends, warning them to leave the party and that someone should notify the cops. Then he steers back onto the road and drives toward our spot, seeming distracted.

"Are you doing okay over there?" I slip off my boots and crack the window open, letting the warm, summer air breeze in.

"What?" He grips the wheel, glancing at me. "Oh yeah, I'm fine." He plasters on a grin. "I mean, why wouldn't I be? I'm with you."

I roll my eyes. "Jesus, if girls heard the shit you said to me, they'd be even more obsessed with you."

"No one's obsessed with me," he says then sighs. "Well, Evalynn is, I guess. But that's different."

"Oh, don't play dumb with me, dude. I know you know almost every girl we went to school with had a crush on you at some point. They weren't obsessing like Evalynn, but a ton of girls think you're hot." I playfully narrow my eyes at him. "And I know you've noticed."

"I do not," he protests. When I give him a don't-try-to-bullshit-me-buddy look, he heaves a dramatic sigh. "Fine, I do. But that doesn't mean I like the attention. In fact, most of the time, I hate it."

Does that apply to Beth too? Considering how much he was smiling at her, I'm going to have to go with a *probably not*. Not that I'm going to say anything.

There's a fine line between teasing your best friend about being a flirt and sounding like a jealous, love-struck stalker.

I pat his arm. "Aw ... poor baby."

"I don't even know why they like me." He grimaces. "I'm not that great."

"Um, yeah, I'm going to have to disagree with you on that."

"Is that your way of trying to say you think I'm great?" he teases with a smirk.

I roll my eyes. "Don't pretend like you don't know you're hot. And sweet. And funny."

His lips span into a grin. "You know, if you keep rolling your eyes like that, they're going to get stuck. Then what am I going to do when I have to send you cryptic looks to get me away from my stalker? You won't be able to see them."

I prop my feet up onto the dash. "Guess you'll just have to come up with another cryptic way to communicate with me."

"Like what exactly?" His tone glitters with amusement. "Cryptically kiss you? Because that doesn't seem very discreet. Although, it'd definitely be interesting."

Sometimes, when he says stuff like that, I worry he's aware that I'm in love with him. But how could he know? I've never told anyone except for Alena. But since I know just as many of her secrets as she does mine, she'd be risking a lot by telling him.

"Let's definitely not do that," I reply, the epitome of chill, but only because I've had practice. Lots and lots of friend-zone practice. "And FYI, not only would us kissing be the lamest way to secretly communicate, but it'd also be the grossest."

"Hey, it could work ..." He trails off, his brows furrowing "Wait. Are you saying you think kissing me would be gross?" He presses his hand to his chest. "Ouch, that kinda stings."

"Dude, don't pretend like you don't agree with me."

"That kissing me is gross?" He stares at the road

ahead. "Yeah, I'm going to disagree with you. In fact, I've been told I'm a fantastic kisser."

So have I, by the handful of girls he's kissed over the years. A few of them are my friends, so I got to hear all the lovely details, and then I pretended to be all *oh my hell, that sounds so amazing*, while a part of my soul withered away.

"I didn't mean you were a bad kisser," I clarify. "I meant you and me kissing would be gross."

He casts me a curious glance. "Why?"

I shrug, reaching for my soda. "I don't know ... Because we've known each other for so long."

I really need to get off this subject before I accidentally say something stupid.

I take a long swallow as I rack my mind for another topic, but he speaks first.

"So, you've never thought about it before?" he asks, watching my reaction closely.

"Thought about kissing you?" I shrug, all awesomely cool on the outside, but I'm a clusterfuck of nerves on the inside. "Not really."

"*Never?*" he questions again.

I shake my head. Why the hell is he pushing this?

He looks back at the road again. "Well, that sucks."

Huh? "Why?"

He fiddles with the stereo. "Because I've thought about it."

"About kissing *me*?"

He has to be messing with me. There's no way Foster could think of me like that. I'd know if he did.

"Yeah." He lowers his hand from the stereo and clears his throat. "A lot actually."

Holy crazy zombies, is this really happening?

Unsure what's going on, I remain quiet. Strangely, so does he. And the silence is beyond awkward, which is annoying. I just got us over this whole silent awkward thing like fifteen minutes ago!

After a minute more of maddening silence, he turns off the highway, driving the short distance down the bumpy dirt road until we reach the parking spot near the cliffs near Hallows Hill. Stretching just in front of us and about thirty feet down is the lake. The water is rippling from the gentle breeze and reflecting in the moonlight. It's such a pretty scene during the day, but at night, this place is gorgeous.

"It's so pretty up here," I remark, reclining back in the seat.

He stays quiet.

When I glance at him, he's looking at me, the moon-light trailing in from the window highlighting the nervous edge in his features.

"You're acting weird," I say. "What's going on in that head of yours?"

"You really want to know?"

The intensity in his eyes makes me hesitate. "I don't know. I guess it all depends on if it's something bad."

He unfastens his seatbelt and twists in the seat to face me. "I don't think it's bad, but you might."

Okay, now I'm getting extremely uneasy. "You're not, like, planning on going off to college and never talk to me again, are you?"

He lets out a soft chuckle. "That's the last thing I'd ever do."

"I highly doubt that," I joke nervously. "There's a ton of stuff I know you'd never do, like pierce your lip, go skydiving, eat a pickle ..." I trail off as he reaches over and touches his palm to my cheek.

He looks me straight in the eye. "I want to kiss you ... I've wanted to for a long time."

Holy did-I-get-high-tonight?

"W-what?" I sputter, feeling a bit lightheaded.

Seriously, did I accidentally get high tonight?

He traces his thumb along my cheekbone. "I've thought about it a lot. I have since I was fourteen. And I know I'm probably freaking you out, and I'm really sorry about it, but I don't think I can do this anymore. That I pretend like I see you as just a friend."

Speechless. That's about what I am. All these years, I thought my feelings for him were one-sided. Come to find out, they weren't. I can't even wrap my mind around it. In fact, I'm pretty sure my brain isn't working at all. I feel so lightheaded. Dizzy. Out of touch with reality.

"I ... I love you."

Oh, my hell! Did I just say that aloud?

I feel ill ...

No... I feel so lightheaded...

Foster exhales, his breath dusting my cheek.

When did he get so close to me?

"I love you, too. So fucking much."

Then he leans across the seat and presses his lips to mine.

The first touch of our lips is gentle, a friendly greeting. But, as he lets out a husky groan and parts my lips with his tongue, that friendly greeting ignites into a deep, four-years-in-the-making passion.

Suddenly, he's kissing me. And I mean, *really* kissing me, his tongue tangling with mine as he tangles his fingers through my hair.

With shaky fingers, I reach down to unfasten my seatbelt so I can get closer to him. It takes me a few tries, mostly because my mind is spinning, but eventually, I manage. Then I clumsily climb over the console, and he eagerly helps me, pulling me over until I'm straddling his lap.

Once I'm settled, he kisses me deeply.

I kiss him with just as much intensity, my lip ring cutting into his lip. He groans in ... in lust? In pure and utter desire? In complete and utter torturous agony? I'm not really sure.

"This is better than I imagined," he whispers when he finally takes a breath.

I nod breathlessly. "Yeah ..."

He plays with my hair, resting his other hand against the sliver of space between my tank top and shorts.

"You really love me?" he asks with his forehead resting against mine.

I bob my head up and down. "I have since I was fifteen." I shut my eyes, feeling so relaxed I could just about fall asleep ...

I'm so dizzy ...

"You should've told me," he murmurs. "All this time, we could've been together."

"That works both ways ... You could've told me, too ..."

Foster leans back to look at me. "I don't want to lose you."

"You won't," I promise.

"Kiss me again," Foster whispers, molding his palm against my cheek.

He doesn't wait for me to answer, his lips finding mine as he slips his hand up my shirt. I don't stop him, even though a protest burns on my tongue.

Hesitant. Why am I hesitant?

And why do I feel so dizzy?

"I love you," he repeats as he trails his fingers toward the waistband of my shorts.

Nervousness creeps up inside me. I've never done anything like this before. But I try to tell myself to calm down. That this is Foster. That everything will be okay.

"I love you," he repeats as he dips his hands down into my shorts. "I'm going to—"

A sharp light cuts off his words.

Then everything goes dark.

SIX
HARLYNN

I'm flying ... Or floating ... I can't really tell. Wherever I am, I feel weightless. Perhaps I turned into a bird or something. But I'm unsure why I would or how I would. Magic maybe?

I start to laugh at the idea that I'm actually considering magic is real when my chest starts to tighten. At first, the sensation is only mildly uncomfortable, but the more the pressure increases, the more the discomfort morphs into pain. And I'm cold. So cold. And wet.

Water. Water is all around me.

Panic flares through my veins, but then the water is no longer there and a darkness eases through me.

"Come on; breathe," a guy's panicked voice cuts through the darkness clouding my mind. "Don't do this. Fight... goddammit."

He sounds brokenly tortured. I want to help him. Want to breathe like he demands. But my lungs aren't working at the moment.

Wait. My lungs aren't working?

I'm not breathing!

Reality crashes down on me, and I attempt to move my body, but just like my lungs, my limbs aren't cooperating.

I'm going to die!

"Come on. Come on ... Don't do this to me." His voice cracks. "Fight. *Please.*"

I want to help him. Want to take his pain away. Want to breathe for him.

I'm trying. I really am.

Warm, familiar lips touch mine.

I think I know those lips ...

Air flows down my throat and feeds my lungs. The pressure builds, tightening, tightening, tightening ... My blood feels thick, heavy, potent, as if it's eating me from the inside out.

I think I'm dying ...

"Come on, please." He sounds like he's crying now. "Please don't give up... I'll do anything."

I want to comfort him, want to make him feel better. So, with every ounce of strength I have left in me, I reach up and brush my fingers through his damp strands of hair.

It'll be all right ...

That's the last thought I have before every noise slips away into the darkness.

Before I slip away into the darkness.

SEVEN

HARLYNN

TWELVE YEARS OLD...

"**K**ingsley's so weird," Foster mutters from beside me.

We're sitting on a dock with our legs dangling over the edge. It's summer, and we've spent the last month doing this exact same thing every day while our families' vacation together. It's becoming a nice routine, just him and me spending lunch away from our parents.

I always invite Kingsley to come with us, but he never does. He hardly ever does anything with us anymore, hasn't since he kissed me on the cheek. I'm not sure why. It was just a kiss on the cheek, and I didn't get upset about it. In fact, it made me feel a lot better after Sprinkles, my fish, died. But, for some reason, he's mad at me now. Maybe because he regrets kissing me? That makes me sort of sad and makes me question if maybe I'm gross or something. None of the boys at school have crushes on me and barely talk to me, so maybe.

I splash my feet in the water, glancing at the cabin porch where Kingsley is reading a book. "I think he's just quiet."

Foster stares at the water with a crinkle at his brow. "He's not as quiet as everyone thinks."

I grip the edge of the dock. "Really?"

He nods. "He talks all the time when we're at home."

"More than you?" I smirk at him.

He narrows his eyes at me, but a smile tugs at his lips. "Just for that." He lightly pushes on my arm, causing me to tip toward the edge.

Panicking, I grip his arm. "Please don't. I suck at swimming."

"Don't worry; I'll jump in and save you." He winks at me.

"Or you could just not push me in," I suggest, latching on to his arm.

He chuckles but stops pushing on me and helps me sit upright again.

I breathe in relief. Not that I believed he'd actually push me in. But just the idea that I could fall in has my heart racing.

Standing up, he offers me his hand. "Let's go up to the rope."

"Fine, but I'm not going to swing on it." I put my hand in his, and he pulls me to my feet.

"Hmm ... that doesn't sound very fun."

"I can't do it. It goes right over the water, and I ..." I toss a panicked glance at the lake. I really hate the water. It's the main reason I don't really know how to swim.

"What if you just swung on it with me?" he suggests, squinting against the sunlight.

I glance at him warily. "I could still fall off."

He shakes his head. "I'd never let that happen." When I give him a skeptical look, he adds, "And even if you fell, I'd fall in with you and swim us to shore."

I flick a glance at the cabin. My mom will never let me go, but she's not outside, so she won't know ...

"Fine. But promise me you'll save me if anything happens." I stick out my pinkie. "In fact, pinkie swear you will."

He hitches his pinkie with mine. "I swear on my life I'll always save you."

"So, you're like my own personal superhero?"

"Totally."

Grinning, we start down the dock toward the shore. Halfway down, Kingsley glances up at us. His gaze lingers on me, again making me question if he hates me.

"I don't think Kingsley likes me," I say right before Foster stumbles on a loose board.

"Shit," Foster says, bumping his shoulder into mine.

Coldness seeps into my bones as I trip sideways. I cry out in pain as my foot gets caught on a nail. Then I lose my footing, tipping over the side of the dock. I gasp right before I plunge in and the water rises over my head. A second later, my toes touch the ground, and I push up with all my might. But the force is only enough to get my head barely above the water, and with my sucky swimming skills—or lack of skills altogether—I sink right back down. The instant my feet touch the ground again, I push back up, and gasp for air as my head surfaces.

"Help," I gasp out, struggling to stay afloat.

I get a brief glimpse of Foster and Kingsley rolling around on the dock, punching each other.

What on earth—

I start to sink again. I try to kick up again, but I don't have enough strength.

Where is Foster? Why is he fighting with Kingsley right now? Why isn't he saving me like he promised?

As I sink lower, I stare up at the sky, at the sunlight sparkling above the water, wondering if this will be the last time I ever see it. Then a shadow falls over me as my feet touch the muddy bottom. Then arms are wound around my waist and I'm pulled upward. A slamming heartbeat later, I burst through the water.

"It's okay. I've got you," Foster assures me as he swims us toward shore.

I cough. "Oh, my gosh, I almost ..." I cling to him and stay that way until we make it safely to the shore.

Foster crawls onto the dirt and smooths my hair out of my face. "Are you okay?"

I flop back in the dirt, struggling to breathe evenly. "Yeah ... I think so ..."

He leans over to examine me, blocking out the sunlight. "Thank God."

I stare up at the sky and drape my hand over my forehead. "I can't believe I fell in. And stepped on a nail, too. My foot's probably bleeding."

"I really need to teach you how to swim better," Foster murmurs, scooting down to look at my foot. "I know you struggle with it, but maybe you can learn how to doggie paddle so you can at least stay afloat if something like that ever happens again." He leans closer to my foot to inspect the wound.

I turn my head toward the dock, and my gaze collides with Kingsley's. He's standing there with his arms crossed and the coldest look on his face.

"Why's Kingsley mad?" I tear my gaze off Kingsley

and look at Foster. "And why were you two fighting while I was in the water?"

Foster sits back, resting his hands on his knees as he glances at Kingsley. "I have no idea what his problem is."

As Foster stares at Kingsley, Kingsley shuts his eyes and shakes his head. Fosters sighs and mutters something incoherently under his breath.

"Are you guys talking telepathically?" I joke.

Foster smiles, but it looks forced. "I was just trying to decide if I should tell you some stuff."

"Like what?"

He rakes his hands through his wet hair then sighs. "It was just so weird ... When you fell in, Kingsley ran over and started punching me. If I didn't know any better, I'd think ..." He shakes his head. "Never mind."

"What is it?" I press. When he shrugs, I softly nudge him in the side of the leg with my foot. "Best friends tell each other everything."

"Yeah, I know, but this might scare you."

"I'm not afraid of anything," I insist. He gives a pressing glance at the water, and I frown. "Well, except for water." I sit up. "But I'm not afraid of Kingsley." I sneak a glance in Kingsley's direction.

He's still on the dock, looking at us miserably.

Why does he look so sad?

"You might be after I tell you this," Foster mutters.

"But I guess I probably should tell you." He turns to me, blocking Kingsley from my view. "When you fell into the lake, he ran over and started punching me, and it was like he was trying to stop me from saving you."

"No way." I shake my head. "He wouldn't do that."

"I'm just telling you how it seemed to me." He sneaks another quick glance over his shoulder at Kingsley then scoots closer to me. "Don't tell anyone I said this, but sometimes it scares me how much he watches you."

I wrap my arms around myself as goosebumps sprout across my skin. "He doesn't watch me that much."

"He kind of does. And I heard my mom and dad talking about how much trouble he's been getting into ... They're starting to get really worried about him. And so am I—"

"Foster! Come help me set up this tent!" his mom shouts from the porch of the cabin.

Grimacing, he stands up. "I'll be right back. Don't go any closer to the water, okay?"

Yeah, I have no problem with that.

He waits for me to nod then jogs off toward the house, leaving his words echoing in my mind.

"No, Kingsley wouldn't try to intentionally hurt me," I mutter to myself.

But when I look back at the dock again and Kingsley

is still staring at me, I can't help wondering if Foster is right.

Why would Kingsley be like that toward me, though? Because he doesn't like me?

I'm not sure, but maybe I should keep my distance from him from now on, just to be safe.

EIGHT
HARLYNN

The soft beeping of a machine tugs me from the darkness. I force my eyelids open, and bright light instantly stings my eyeballs. For a frightening moment, I think I'm dead. But then the light gradually dims and my surroundings slowly come into focus.

An off-white ceiling, florescent lights, and plain white walls? *Where the hell am I?*

I glance around. I'm in a bed with an IV tube in my hand, an oxygen tube is underneath my nose, and my finger is connected to a heart monitor.

I'm in a hospital?

Sharp images flash through my mind. Foster's truck. Kissing him. A bright light. After that ... nothing.

"Oh, good, you're awake." A middle-aged woman wearing blue scrubs enters the room, carrying a clipboard.

"Um, yeah?" I peer around the empty room. "Where're my parents?"

"They went to the cafeteria." She approaches the bed. "Your poor mother's been worried sick about you, refusing to leave your bedside even to eat, but your father finally convinced her to go. Figures you'd wake up the moment she left. Things usually seem to work out that way, don't they?"

I stare at her, confused, but she just offers me a small smile.

"Let's check your vitals, shall we?" She examines the monitor screen then jots down something on the clipboard.

"How long have I been here?" I ask hoarsely, my throat dry and scratchy.

"About a week." She sets the clipboard down on a table and pours me a glass of water, adding a straw to the cup. "You've been in and out of consciousness most of the time."

"Really? I don't remember that." I take the cup from her and gulp down a long sip.

"You were fairly incoherent. But you seem all right now. Your vitals look a lot better."

I drink the last of the water then hand her back the cup. "Why? What happened to me?"

Her optimism goes *poof*. "You don't remember?" she

asks cautiously.

I shake my head. "I remember being in a truck with my friend ..." And making out with him, but I'm not about to tell her that. "Then there was a bright light. After that, I can't remember anything except waking up here." When she frowns, I ask, "Is it bad I can't remember?"

She forces a rigid smile. "I'm sure it's fine, but let me just go get the doctor, okay?"

She shuffles out of the room, leaving me with nothing but the beeping of the heart machine and my confusion to keep me company.

I stare down at my hands, at my bandaged wrist.

What happened to me? Why can't I remember anything after when Foster and I kissed in the truck? Did I get hurt right after that? How? And where's Foster?

"Did he get hurt, too?" I mumble as I move to sit up, but my head gets yanked back by the oxygen tube. "Fuck."

My mom steps into the doorway and her hand trembles as she covers her mouth. "Oh, you're awake."

"Calm down, honey." My dad wraps his arms around her. "Take a deep breath. Air in. Air out."

She does what he says, taking deep breaths. Then she hurries over to my bedside.

Her eyes glisten with tears as she smooths her hand over my head. "How are you feeling? Does anything hurt? Do you need anything? Food? Water? Another blanket?"

She pulls back, but only to pick up the buzzer. "You know what? I'm just going to buzz the nurse."

"She's already been here. She just left to go find the doctor," I tell her. "Mom, calm down. I'm fine."

She reluctantly lets go of the buzzer. "You're not fine. You were hurt, and we thought ..." She shakes her head, a sob ripping from her chest.

"Hon, you're scaring Harlynn." My dad places his hand over mine, his eyes looking a bit watery, too. "God, I'm so glad you're okay."

Good hell, am I the only stable one in this room? If so, it's a bit unsettling since I'm currently hooked up to oxygen.

"We're sorry we're so emotional," my dad apologizes to me, dabbing his eyes with the sleeve of his shirt. "We were just so worried you wouldn't wake up."

My heart rate spikes. "I was in a coma?"

"No, but you were in and out of consciousness. And every time you woke up ..." He trails off, tears welling in his eyes again.

"You didn't recognize us," my mom finishes for him as she sucks in a trembling breath. "But that's okay. You recognize us now ..." She pauses, assessing me closely. "Right?"

"Yes, Mom, I know who you are," I assure her. "And I know who Dad is. I know my name, my birthday, where I live ... I'm fine. I swear." I glance down at my arm, at a bandage wrapped around my wrist, and haziness floods my mind. *How did I hurt it?* "I'm a little confused about something ... How I ended up in a hospital..."

"You don't remember?" my mom asks. When I shake my head, she looks like she's going to lose it. "Doug, go get the doctor now."

"Don't do that, Dad," I say, but he's already rushing out of the room.

Sighing, I return my attention to my mom. "I already said the nurse went to get the doctor."

"Well, she's moving too slowly." She pulls up a chair, sits down, and then holds my hand. "I know you like to be tough, but you were in a serious car accident, and we need to be one hundred percent certain you're okay. No sugar-coating your answers when the doctor asks you questions, got it?"

"I'll do my best, but ... Wait ... I was in a car accident?" My mind flashes back to the last memory I had. *I was in Foster's truck with him ...* "Where's Foster?" I try to sit up, but that damn oxygen tube gets in the way again. "Goddammit, this thing is so annoying." I reach to yank it off.

"Don't you dare," my mom warns, capturing my hand. "You need to leave that on until the doctor takes it off."

"Fine." I lower my hand to my lap. "Is Foster okay?"

She pats my hand and smiles at me. "Other than a couple of bruises and cuts, he's fine. But considering what happened ... things could've been a lot worse."

I swallow hard. "What happened exactly?"

"From what Foster told us, you two were parked out on Hallows Hill near the lake when someone crashed into the back of his truck." She takes a shaky breath then scoots forward on the chair. "His truck was pushed over the cliff and it fell into the lake."

I can't breathe ...

So much water ...

Help me ...

Warm lips on mine, feeding me air ...

I know those lips ...

"Harlynn, are you okay?"

I blink, yanking myself out of my daze. "Yeah ..." I blink again as the broken images simmer and fizzle inside my mind. "How did I get out of the lake?"

"Foster pulled you out and swam you to shore." She offers me a weary smile. "I always knew I liked that boy."

Foster saved me again?

Warm lips on mine ...

I know those lips ...

From somewhere ...

Somewhere faint and distant yet familiar...

"I ..." I rub at my eyes with the heels of my hands,

trying to rub away the confusion. "Who ran into Foster's truck?"

"No one knows for sure since the person who hit you took off. The police are looking into it, but it's been labeled as a potential hit and run."

"Do they think it was an accident, or did they hit us on purpose?" I'm not sure why the question slips past my tongue. As far as I know, Foster has very few enemies. Well, except for Grey. But this is a little bit extreme for Grey and Foster's rivalry.

"We don't know yet," my mom utters, clutching my hand. "We'll have to wait to hear from the police. Until then, we've been cautioned for everyone to be extra careful and report anything strange that we might've seen or heard." She tightens her grip on mine. "The detective in charge of the case has requested to speak to you about what happened when you're feeling up to it."

Images flash through my mind.

A bright light. A loud crash.

Warm lips on mine ...

My head starts to throb.

My mom glances at the monitor as my heart rate increases. I tug on her hand, drawing her attention back to me.

"I'm okay," I lie.

I'm not sure I am.

I feel different inside. There's a hollowness stirring inside me, a blankness of lost time.

The corners of my mom's lips dip downward even more. "I'll feel better after the doctor checks on you."

Me, too. Then maybe they can explain why I can't recall much of anything about the wreck.

"When can I see Foster?" I ask.

"I'm sure he'll be by soon," she tells me. "He stops in at least four to five times a day to check up on you. He'd probably stay here all the time if he could."

I nod, but my mind feels so foggy.

Foster saved me. Foster, the guy I've been in love with. The guy I kissed right before the accident.

I wish I could remember ...

Why can't I?

NINE

HARLYNN

The doctor, a thirty-something-year-old woman, shows up a little later to check on me. Her name is Dr. Paratellford, and her hair reminds me of blood.

After asking me only a couple of questions and giving me a quick examination, she decides my memory loss is probably due to the traumatic event.

"We've already done an MRI, and it showed no brain trauma." She tucks a pen into her front pocket and adjusts the clipboard in her hand. "So, more than likely, it's from the traumatic stress of the event."

"So, traumatic stress is causing the memory loss?" I ask.

She nods, glancing down at my chart. "It's not that uncommon, especially if you reached a state of shock before you passed out."

"Oh, I'm sure Harlynn did," my mom tells the doctor. "She hates water."

I nod in agreement. "I do." That much is still true.

What I don't understand, though, is why my memory blanks out even before Foster's truck went off the cliff. Even the memories of making out with Foster are a bit hazy, as if they didn't really happen. Everyone keeps saying it's from the trauma, but why would I forget a memory that was so important to me? Or, well, it feels like it should be. Right now, I just feel... Well, like I'm floating around in a sea encompassed by fog.

"We'll keep her here for a couple more days for observation," the doctor tells my parents. "But if everything looks okay by then, she'll be able to go home."

My parents start asking her with questions about when they do take me home. During the chat my mom mentions Foster had to do mouth-to-mouth on me, that my lungs actually stopped seeking air.

I died for a moment.

Dead.

I was dead.

And now I'm here, alive, and all I feel is confused.

After the doctor leaves the room, my dad calls the Avertonsons to let them know I'm awake, doing okay, and that they can come over to visit me. When he gets off the phone, he informs us that they're heading over ASAP.

I'm unsure how I feel about this. I feel as if I should be excited to see Foster, but I don't think I am. Honestly, all I feel is exhausted.

I will my eyelids to stay open, but they start to lower. I try to fight the sleepiness, fight going into the darkness, a bit of fear seeping through that I'll never wake up again. And while fear isn't usually a welcomed emotion, I'm glad to feel something other than confusion.

"It's okay, sweetie." My mom kisses my forehead as I struggle to keep my eyes open. "You can rest. The doctor said you'll probably be a bit sleepy over the next few days."

I shake my head from side to side. "I'm not tired at all."

"Go to sleep." My mom smooths her hand over my head. "You need your rest."

I don't want to rest. I feel like that's all I've been doing. Resting. Deep, deep asleep in a world full of darkness. And now I feel restless to stay awake. Yet, I'm somehow tired. I'm a contradiction. I was dead, and now I'm alive. And now there are holes in my memory, like empty graves waiting to be filled.

I feel so strange...

"Go to sleep, sweetie," my mom repeats. "You'll be fine."

Sighing, I let my eyelids close and surrender to the darkness, falling into a dream of a memory.

TEN
HARLYNN

Do you ever get the feeling your life is just one big, pathetic tragedy? I do almost every single day. Not that I don't have a good life. My parents love me and, for the most part, they don't get too upset with me when I screw up. I've always had a roof over my head and have never gone hungry. I'm decent at school and have stuff I'm good at, like writing and running. One of my short stories was published in the school newspaper, and I have friends.

So, yeah, on the outside, my life is good. It's the inside that's the tragedy. Because I've fallen in love with my best friend who will only ever see me as a friend. And, while I've tried time and time again to stop loving him, I can't seem to convince my heart to let go. Instead, it's stuck its claws into that love and left me struggling to deal with it.

Usually, I'm pretty good at keeping my feelings hidden, but today, my façade is rapidly withering.

It all started when Zoey, one of the most popular girls in school, invited Foster to a party. Normally, Foster gets an invite for me as well, but he must have forgotten this time, something I realize the more he talks about the party.

"I heard there was going to be a band there," he says, fiddling with the stereo.

School just ended, and we're in his truck, getting ready to pull out of the parking lot.

"Sounds like it'll be awesome," I say, fastening my seatbelt.

"For sure," he agrees. "Now, if I can just find us a DD, I'll be good to party all night long." He sings the last part and laughs.

When he says us, I think he means him and me, so I start to smile. He didn't forget about me. But then he adds, "I invited Ana to the party, and you know how she gets. A DD is a must."

My smile falters. Ana. He invited Ana? But he told me the other day she annoys him.

"I thought you didn't like Ana." I dig my phone out from my pocket as it buzzes with an incoming text.

"She's okay," he hesitantly replies then shrugs. "I mean, I don't not like her. Plus, she has a hot ass." He throws me a teasing grin, causing my lips to twitch.

"You know I'm not a guy, right? I'm not going to high-five you over a girl's ass."

"It'd be cool if you did, though." He grins, but then he sighs when I don't return it. "Hey, I'm sorry, okay? I'll try not to talk about hot asses around you anymore ... unless it's a guy's hot ass." He grins, and my lips start to turn upward until he adds, "Hey, you should be my DD. You can come hang out at the party then give me and Ana a ride home when we're ready to go."

My first instinct is to tell him yes. That's what I usually do. But I hesitate. I'm not sure why. Maybe because I don't feel like being the DD again. Or perhaps because it feels like he's only telling me to go to the party to be his DD and honestly, I've never really been a huge fan of the parties we go to—I just go because I like spending time with him. Or perhaps I'm just being bitter that he's going out with Ana and not me.

"You good with that?" He rests his arm on the windowsill as he steers out of the parking space.

"I don't know ..." My willpower withers as he looks at me with his puppy dog eyes.

"Com on, Har," he begs. "I'll love you forever."

"Oh, fine ..." I trail off as my phone buzzes again.

I glance down at the screen and see I've received two messages from Star, a girl in my English class who loves reading and writing just as much as I do. She also dyes her hair blood red, wears a lot of black, and has a ton of piercings. Sometimes, I wonder why we're not better friends, since we have a lot in common. But Star isn't a fan of preppy jocks, and Foster and a lot of our mutual friends are the definition of that, so maybe that's why. Or maybe it's because she sometimes hangs out with Porter and Kingsley and it's kind of an unsaid rule that friends of Kingsley's are off limits for people who are friends with Foster.

Star: Hey, crazy girl, I thought I'd let you know the deets about the party I told you about, just in case you change your mind about coming.

Star: It's going to be wicked fun. There's a live band playing, and they're really good.

I turned down her offer to the party because of who her friends are and also because I assumed Foster and I were going to be doing something tonight. But you know what they say about assuming? Apparently, I'd forgotten that motto. I'm painfully starting to remember it now.

"Earth to Har." Foster lightly tugs on a strand of my hair. "Where's your head at?"

I shrug. "In La La Land."

He chuckles, flipping on the blinker. "Isn't it always there?"

"Most of the time. In fact, I'm thinking of applying for residency soon."

He grins as we roll up to a stop sign. "Sounds like the perfect plan, just as long as I get to visit you."

His smile is contagious, and I start to smile myself.

"I think I'll—"

"Wait. Hold that thought." He holds up a finger then glances at his phone. "It's Ana. She wants to know if I found us a DD." He looks at me expectantly. "You're good with me telling her yes, right?" He starts to reach for his phone without waiting for me to reply.

Something snaps inside me.

Breaks.

And is replaced by a very strong frustration that sizzles and burns through my veins.

"Actually, I have other plans," I say, surprising myself.

Before I can back out, I send Star a message.

Me: You know what? I'm in.

Foster's brows rise in surprise. "Seriously?"

"Yes, seriously." I cross my arms and slump back in the chair, staring out the window. "I do have a life, despite what you think."

"Hey, I'm sorry if something I said upset you."

"You didn't do anything," I lie, glancing at him. "I'm just bummed I'm going to miss the party."

He eyes me over. "What're you doing tonight?"

"Helping my mom clean out the attic," I lie again. I do

it so easily, too, and it makes me question what kind of person I am.

Who lies to their best friend without even second-guessing the decision? Have I always been like this?

"That sucks. Your attic's a mess." He pulls out onto the road. "If you get done early, maybe you can still come to the party."

"Maybe." I glance down at my phone as another message pings through.

Star: Awesome. You want a ride?

Me: Sure. As long as it's not out of the way for you.

Star: I'm actually riding with someone else, but they're cool with picking you up.

"If you do decide to come, let me know," Foster says. "I'd rather you be my DD than some dude Ana knows."

"Yeah, I'll let you know." But I make a vow to myself right then and there not to go to that party. I'm going to do my own thing tonight without having to watch the guy I'm in love with be with someone else again.

I don't say much for the rest of the ride home, something Foster notices and asks about several times. I attempt not to be pissy and tell him I'm fine, but it's obvious I'm in a sullen mood.

"You sure you're okay?" he asks as he parks in my driveway.

Nodding, I shove open the door and hop out. "Have fun tonight. And be safe."

He smiles but his forehead creases as he glances at my house. The lights are off inside, and it looks extremely dark with the cloudy, stormy sky above.

"It looks like no one's home," he states. "Are you sure you have to stay home and clean the attic tonight?"

"Yep. My mom will be home soon." I move to shut the door.

"Har, wait," he calls out, and I pause. He rakes his fingers through his hair, making the strands go askew. "Are you mad at me or something?"

"No." It's the truth, too. If I'm mad at anyone, it's myself for falling in love with a guy who clearly isn't going to ever see me as more than a friend. "Have fun tonight." I wave at him then close the door, turn around, and hike up the path to the single-story home I grew up in.

Foster lives a few blocks down the road. Our parents have had a ton of barbeques with each other, thrown joint birthday parties, and celebrated the holidays together. Foster and I were always there, hanging out together, opening presents, laughing, pulling pranks, and when we got older, sometimes we snuck a few beers and drink in the basement. Almost every memory I have is with him, because I've spent every second I could with him. And now I'm here, alone with no plans of seeing him tonight, and I feel ... weird. But not necessarily in a bad way.

Honestly, I feel sort of free. Free from suffering through another one-sided night of love. But that doesn't mean I feel bad about lying to Foster. I do. A lot. In fact, I feel so terrible that, for the next few hours while I'm getting ready for the party, I almost text him several times to retract my answer about not going to the party and being his DD. But I never fully get there, and before I know it, Star is texting me.

Star: Are you ready to go? Your chariot has arrived.

Me: Yep! Heading outside now.

I give a quick glance in the mirror. My long, brown hair that has streaks of violet in it is swept to the side in a mess of waves and braids. I decided to wear an off-the-shoulder, black velvet top and paired it with cut-offs, fishnets, and clunky boots so I'm a little bit fancy and a little bit grungy. I kept my makeup minimal, sticking with my normal kohl eyeliner and lip gloss look. Still, I think I look okay. Decent even.

As a horn honks from the driveway, I yank my gaze off the mirror and hurry out of my room. My mom and dad are gone on a date, so I don't have to explain where I'm going looking more dressed up than I normally do, and where I'm going without Foster.

Grabbing my set of house keys and some cash, I step outside, a bit excited. Of course, when I spot the beat-up Cadillac parked in the driveway, most of my enthusiasm fizzles.

Star rode with Porter. Awesome.

"Hurry your cute ass up!" Star hollers from out the window.

As I near the car, I can see she's sitting in the back by herself, Porter is in the driver's seat, and sitting in the passenger seat is ...

Kingsley.

"Shit," *I mutter under my breath. Why did I not think about this before? I know she sometimes hangs out with them. It should've crossed my mind at least once that maybe they were going to be with her tonight.*

I force myself to keep walking forward.

Don't be rude. You'll be fine. It's just one car ride.

"You look cute." Star leans over the seat and sticks her head out of the rolled down passenger side window.

I smile. "So do you."

She does, too, with her hair down and curled in wild waves, her lips are stained red, and her eyelids are covered in glitter.

"And we all know I look sexy as hell." Porter throws me a grin.

I roll my eyes. "That wasn't the words I was going to use."

"Handsome as fuck?" he offers, his grin widening.

"Not even close. In fact, I was thinking the exact opposite." I smirk then sneak a glance at Kingsley.

He's engulfed with his phone, tapping buttons with a crease between his brows.

"Dude, stop." Porter snatches Kingsley's phone away from him and chucks it in the console. "No more phones for the night."

Kingsley cuts his gaze to him. "Are you being serious right now?"

Porter smirks. "I'm always fucking serious."

"Yeah right," Star and I say simultaneously then laugh. "Jinx!" we both call out then laugh again. "Jinx, jinx, jinx!"

Star swats my arm. "Stop trying to jinx me."

"You stop trying to jinx me," I say through my laughter.

"Will you both stop trying to jinx each other so Harlynn can get her cute ass in the car? I've got big plans for this party." Porter smirks at me as I glare at him.

Kingsley shakes his head, thrumming his fingers on top of his knee. "Of course you do. You're a drama queen."

When I smile at that, Kingsley cracks a tiny smile in

return. Then he chews on his bottom lip, studying me undecidedly.

"You want me to let you in?" he finally asks.

"No, she wants you to make her stand out there until it rains," Star quips. "Of course she wants in, dumbass."

Kingsley shoots her a playful dirty look then opens the door. I may be tall, but Kingsley has always made me feel short, his height resting somewhere around six-foot-four or so.

Foster is a couple of inches shorter than him and doesn't make me feel quite as small. And he doesn't make me feel as intimidated either.

Kingsley gives me a quick once-over as he hops out then turns around, frowning as he shoves the seat forward.

Great. Did I overdress or something?

I discreetly check out their outfits. Porter is sporting dark jeans and a black T-shirt, along with a studded belt and gauges are in his ears. Kingsley is rocking his typical all black attire, with leather bands on his wrists and chains dangling from his belt loop. And Star has on a red velvet dress and lace-up boots.

No, I'm pretty sure I look fine. Maybe Kingsley is just annoyed I'm going with them. But, oh well. He'll have to get over it, because I spent way too much time convincing myself to go to this party and I'm not backing out now.

Squaring my shoulders, I swing around Kingsley and lower my head to get into the back seat.

"You look nice," he mutters softly.

"Um ... thanks?" I sound as perplexed as I feel. But I seriously think that might be the first nice thing he's said to me since he kissed me on the cheek all those years ago.

"Aw, look, he does know how to be sweet," Star teases as I drop down onto the seat beside her.

Kingsley scowls at her, but the corners of his lips twitch upward. Then he turns around, slides into the passenger seat, and shuts the door.

For most of my life, Kingsley has acted either sad or angry. Never joking. Apparently, he's different around his friends. I wonder why. Because he doesn't like Foster? Because he doesn't like me? Do I really care if he does? After all, I made a promise to myself after the day I fell into the lake that I'd keep my distance from him.

Of course, here I am, breaking that promise.

"So, I feel like I should warn you about a couple of things," Star tells me, flipping her hair off her shoulder.

"Okay, what's up?"

"Well, for starters, don't drink anything at this party. And don't smoke anything either."

"Okay ...?" Confusion swirls through me. I mean, it's not like I have to get high or drunk every time I go to parties, but what she said seems weird.

She must read the puzzlement on my face since she adds, "Don't worry; we're totally going to pre-party in the car."

I frown. "While we're driving?"

She shakes her head. "Nah, we'll park at the party, then pre-party in here before we go in."

"Oh." How ... weird.

"You look so confused."

"I'm not," I lie. I totally am. And I feel like a loser because I am.

She trades a look with Porter then Kingsley, making me feel like the butt of a private joke.

I never should've done this. I don't fit in with them.

Sometimes I feel like I don't fit in with anyone.

"Relax." Star pats my leg. "You'll have fun. I promise."

"I'm not doubting the fun part. It just seems weird we're going to party it up in the car before we go to the party. And, why can't I drink or smoke anything while I'm there? Do people, like, drug drinks and stuff?" Because, if so, then I don't think I want to go.

"No, James—the ... dude throwing the party—has a no drinking and drugs policy at his house to avoid that problem," she explains. "He's cool with people drinking and smoking before they arrive, though. We're just not allowed to bring anything in with us. And he'll kick out anyone

who does, so if someone offers you something, don't touch it, okay?"

"That's cool. I can totally respect that." It still sounds a bit weird, though.

"Of course you can." Porter tosses me a smirk from over his shoulders. "Because you're a fucking saint, right? In fact, I bet you've never even been fucking drunk or high, especially with how much you hang out with Foster, who thinks he's a fucking saint, even though he's not."

What? Is fuck his favorite word or something? Or is he just trying to make himself seem more bad boyish?

"Actually, you're wrong," I cut in. "I may not party all the time, but I'm not a fucking saint, and Foster doesn't think he's a fucking saint either. But, even if I was a fucking saint, it's none of your guys' fucking business." I flash Porter the same haughty smirk he always gives me.

His eyes darken in delight, and then he cocks a brow at Kingsley. "Okay, maybe I do get it now."

Kingsley gives him a dirty look then cautiously glances at me. "Does my brother know where you're going tonight?"

"Sure," I lie. "Why?"

His gaze bores into me. "Does he know who you're with?"

"He knows I'm with Star," I lie again.

"Are you going to tell him you're with Porter and me?" he asks, his gaze relentless.

"I don't know, probably." Another lie leaves my tongue.

Man, I'm on a roll today, aren't I?

"Maybe you should tell him now," Porter suggests, watching me from the rearview mirror. "You know, just in case you want to leave the party early."

"She'll be fine." Star scoots forward and rests her arms on the console. "You two need to chill out. You're scaring off a potential friend."

Kingsley's gaze glides to her. They stare each other down for a few seconds before he sighs and looks forward again.

"Fine," he mutters. "But she's your responsibility."

My jaw ticks. "I'm not a child. I don't need anyone to be responsible for me."

"The fact that you can say that means you do," Kingsley mumbles, hunkering down in the seat and putting his knees against the dashboard.

As anger simmers underneath my skin, I reach over the seat and flick him in the back of the head. "Quit being an asshole."

He snaps his hand back to where I flicked him, lowers his feet to the floor, and then rotates in the seat toward me. "Did you just flick me on the head?" He gapes at me.

I lift a shoulder, but my heart is racing in my chest. "Yeah, so what if I did?"

His lips part, but he hurriedly presses them together then turns back around in the seat, remaining silent for the rest of the drive. When we reach the party, he bails out of the car before Porter even comes to a full stop.

"Man, he's moody tonight," Star says as she unfastens her seatbelt.

Porter glances at her with his brow arched. "I wonder why."

It doesn't go unnoticed that his gaze briefly strays in my direction. Then he silences the engine and hops out of the car.

"He doesn't want me here, does he?" I mutter as I flip the seat forward. "Kingsley, I mean."

Star wavers. "It's not that. I think he's just nervous."

Kingsley nervous? That doesn't even seem like a thing? "Why is he nervous?"

She shrugs then puts on a smile. "You know what? Let's have some fun." She pulls out a bottle of vodka and doesn't say anything further about Kingsley. But she doesn't have to.

It's pretty damn clear he doesn't want me here.

ELEVEN
HARLYNN

I wake up feeling groggy and lightheaded. Chatter is buzzing in the air, along with the beeping of the heart monitor.

"I'm so glad she woke up," Janie Avertonson says, the relief in her tone evident.

"Me, too. For a second ..." My mom chokes up.

"It's going to be okay," Janie reassures her. "Come on; let's take a walk and get some fresh air."

It grows quiet after that, so I open my eyes and glance around, expecting to be alone. But Foster is sitting in a chair beside my bed. He has his phone out, his gaze is fixed on the screen, and his brows are creased. He has a bandage on the back of his hand, a healing cut on his forehead, and a bruise is splattered across his cheek. Wounds he got from the accident, I'm guessing.

Sighing, he shakes his head and puts his phone away, lifting his gaze. His eyes briefly widen then a smile breaks across his face. "Hey, you're awake." He stands up and hurries to my bedside. "God, I've missed those pretty eyes."

"That was pretty cheesy," I attempt to tease, but my voice sounds hoarse and scratchy. "Can you get me some water?"

"Of course." He pours me some, hands me the cup, then smiles. "How're you feeling? Your mom said you were okay, but she also said your memory of what happened is hazy."

I take a sip of water. "Yeah, I can't remember much of what happened after your truck was hit. But word on the street is you're the reason I'm here."

He sinks down on the edge of the bed and smooths my hair from my eyes. "It's not a big deal."

I search his face, seeking answers, longing for a memory to surface of what happened that night, but ... *nothing*.

"What happened? All I remember is being in the truck with you and ... that's about it. Well, other than waking up in a hospital bed."

He places a hand on each side of my head. "Do you remember us kissing in my truck?"

I nod, expecting my heart to flutter at the memory, but

it remains quiet. "Yeah, a little bit of it anyway."

"Do you remember how we said I love you to each other?" he asks, and I nod again. "Good, then let's leave it at that." He tucks a lock of my hair behind my ear. "It's better if you don't remember what happened after that. It was ... awful."

I nod, but the movement feels robotic. I want to know —need to know—so I can place his face to the faint memories I have of being saved, place his face to that begging voice, the one that pleaded with me to come back, to not die, that they'd do anything if I didn't.

Warm lips on mine ...

Breathing air into me ...

I died for an instant. Stopped breathing.

Air left my lungs, and my heart stood motionless inside my chest, just like I feel now.

Panic trickles through me, and the heart monitor's beeping accelerates.

Worry creases Foster's face as he glances at the screen then back at me. "Har, relax." He strokes his fingers across my cheek. "Everything's going to be okay. You're fine. I'm fine. Everyone is fine."

I nod, but the panic stays. I feel so different, as if I'm not myself anymore. A few days ago, the sight of him would've made my stomach flutter and my heart dance to life, but now I feel nothing but confusion.

"I'm sorry," I say. "It's just weird having blank spots in my memories."

"That's understandable. But, like I said, it's probably better if you don't remember. I wish I couldn't ... Wish that I couldn't remember seeing you that way ... I'm just really glad you're okay." He kisses my cheek. "I don't know what I'd do without you. I can't ever lose you."

I wait for his kiss to bring me warmth, but coldness drapes over me.

"I can't ever lose you either." I pretend I'm telling the truth, that I can't feel a hint of doubt swimming inside me. Doubt. So much doubt. That's all I am right now. Is this because of the memory loss? If so, I need to remember so I can feel like my normal self again. "It's going to suck when you leave for school."

He kisses my cheek again then leans back. "I know." He traces a path down my hairline. "I've talked to our parents, and they think it'll be good for us if you come and visit me on the weekends."

Us, like we're a couple.

I feel as though I should be giddy, but confusion webs through me. Are we dating now? We never discussed this. Not that I don't want to date him.

I think ...

What the hell is wrong with me?

"I'd like that. But I have to make sure I can get work off."

"I'm sure it'll be fine. Your boss is pretty chill, right?"

"Yeah." The truth is that I need the money from my job for school, and I don't want to drive twelve hours every weekend. It just seems so far. And so ... Well, I'm not really sure. "But you said you'd come up here on the weekends."

He scrunches his nose. "I'd rather you come and visit me. I mean, think about it." He holds his hands up to the side of him. "We can hang out here, in one of our parents' houses, and spend our time hanging out with the same people we've seen every single day of our lives." He lowers one of his hands slightly and lifts the other. "Or you can come to my place, and we can go to parties unsupervised and meet new people."

Meet new people? It's like he doesn't know me at all. And he's being so pushy.

Has he always been like this?

"I guess I'll see if I can get the time off." I force a smile. But he doesn't seem to notice. Or doesn't care.

"Awesome." Smiling, he leans over and places a soft kiss to my lips.

Warm lips on mine ...

Breathing air into my lungs ...

So soft ...

So full ...

So different from the lips that are touching mine right now.

I jerk back, my heart rate quickening for a split-second before settling right back down.

Foster sits back, his gaze darting from the monitor to me. "What's wrong?"

"Nothing." I stare at him. And I mean, *really* stare at him.

I stare at him for so long that he starts to look at me like I'm losing it.

"You gave me mouth-to-mouth that night, right?" I ask.

"I did, and it was one of the worst moments of my life ... For a second, I thought ..." He swallows hard. "Can we please not talk about this? I still have nightmares over seeing you like that."

Warm lips on mine.

Not Foster's lips...

I'm pretty sure Foster didn't give me mouth-to-mouth.

I'm pretty sure he's lying.

But then, who saved me?

My mind spins with dizziness as I struggle to piece together what happened.

Maybe I'm just being weird. Maybe the crash left me

insane. Maybe some of my sanity got lost with my memories.

Maybe I'm really dead and this is my hell.

"Har ..." Foster starts but trails off as our parents enter the room.

I feel relieved by the interruption.

Relieved that I can avoid the truth for a little bit.

And the truth is that I'm fairly sure Foster just lied to me.

TWELVE
HARLYNN

A few days later, after the doctor has run a couple of tests and they all come back okay, I'm released from the hospital. My memories of the accident, though, remain hazy at best. According to the doctor, they may eventually return to me, but maybe not. Only time will tell.

A couple of days after I go home, my mom takes me to get a new phone since mine is probably somewhere at the bottom of the lake. Then we go to the police station so I can fill out a form on what I can remember about the night of the accident. Needless to say, I'm not much help.

"If you can remember anything else at all, don't hesitate to call me," the officer working on the case says to me as she hands me her card.

She's in her late thirties, has chin-length black hair,

and seems nice enough, especially considering how unhelpful I've been.

I stuff the card into my pocket. "Okay, I will."

She smiles then turns to my mom. "Can I speak to you alone for a second? There's some things I'd like to discuss."

"Oh, um, sure." My mom turns to me. "Can you wait for me by the chairs near the entrance. The car is locked."

I could point out that she could just give me the key, but she's been acting really weird about me being alone ever since the accident. So I nod and wander out into the main part of the station. The air buzzes with energy, phones are ringing, and an officer is hauling some guy in. All the noise starts to make my head ache so I walk to the front section of the station where it's a bit quieter and start to sit down in a chair.

But then I hear a whisper.

"Look at the back wall."

My gaze darts over my shoulder. I expect someone to be behind me, but no one other than the woman sitting at the front counter is around, and she's on the phone.

So weird.

Still, I find myself looking at the back wall. It's covered with missing person's flyers. I inch toward it, my gaze landing on one flyer in particular.

Paige Meriforter.

I knew Paige from school. She was a year older than me, and I sometimes talked to her during art class. She was the kind of girl who hardly anyone noticed until she vanished. Then she was all anyone could talk about, her absence giving her the popularity she once told me she craved.

Since her parents were drug addicts, her home life was shit, and she took a bunch of cash and her mom's car with her when she disappeared, almost everyone assumed she just ran away.

Maybe she did. Perhaps she's living somewhere in some big city, happy to be away from Sunnyvale and her shitty life. But I don't know, looking at this flyer, I get the strangest feeling that Paige is still in town. And close.

"Are you ready to go?" my mom asks from behind me.

I blink from the flyer and twist around to face her. "Sure."

We walk out of the station and get into the car, my mind filled with the weird thought I had about Paige.

"What did the detective want to talk to you about?" I ask my mom in an attempt to distract myself from thoughts of Paige.

She forces a small smile. "She just wanted to make sure that if you do remember anything else about the accident, that we'll let her know." She clutches the steering wheel as she lets out an unsteady exhale. "I knew you couldn't remember much, but I didn't realize you couldn't even remember stuff about before the truck went off the cliff." She glances over at me. "You weren't drinking that night, were you?"

"No." It's the first truth I've told in a while and go figure, she doesn't appear to fully believe me. But she doesn't say anything else.

I internally sigh, wishing I could remember. Maybe then, everyone would stop acting so careful around me, like I'm cracked glass about to break apart.

But that's not the only reason I want to remember. No, I'm still not convinced Foster was the one who gave me mouth-to-mouth. But it doesn't make sense why Foster would lie about saving me. He was there that night, though, in the truck with me. That much I remember. How we kissed. How we declared our love to each other. Yet, those memories are cloudy, like I was fading in and out of time.

Honestly, I still feel like I am.

THIRTEEN
HARLYNN

A couple of days later, I'm stretched out on my bed and writing in my journal, trying to write the truth from my mind. Music is blasting from the stereo, the song the type of music Foster and my parents give me crap about for listening to.

What happened to me when I went into the water?

When darkness swam around me, stabbing at my limbs and mind?

When my lungs singed with death, and my heart drowned in the agony of stillness?

Why do I still feel so confused, like I'm walking around in a fog?

I drop my pen and massage my temples with my fingertips as my head begins to throb, something that's been happening a lot lately. I continue massaging until the dull ache goes away. Then I lower my hands from my head, push up, and scoot to the edge of the bed, trying to figure out what to do next.

I've been home for three days now and haven't done much of anything except lie around in bed, streaming movies, writing in my journal, and sleeping. Dirty clothes cover my floor, along with books and shoes. I'm not a neat freak or anything, but this place is a mess compared to how it usually is.

Everyone said I should take it easy, and I've been doing what I've been told, despite this restlessness stirring inside me, telling me to go figure out what in the hell happened to me the night of the accident. The problem is I have no idea how to do that other than to get the details from Foster, but so far, he's been no help at all.

Plus, I haven't seen much of him since I returned home. In the past, I'd be bummed about that and would've gone over to help him pack like he's asked me to a few times. But I haven't had much desire to see him other than the brief moments where I've considered going over there to demand he tell me the truth, so I can finally see through this constant fog haunting my mind.

Haunted. I feel so haunted by something I can't even begin to describe.

Lowering my hands from my temples, I reach for my laptop and open up the webpage I've been reading. It's an article about near-death experiences and what happens to people after they're brought back to life. I've been reading in an attempt to figure out if maybe my memory loss and confusion is a side effect of that. A lot of weird stuff has pulled up, from people believing they can see the future to some even believing they can now travel to the afterlife once they've died and returned to life. Some speak of memory loss and feel differently, almost like they came back a different person, the person they were always supposed to be. That their near-death experience was like someone had pulled a veil off their eyes.

Is that what's happening to me? Is this who I was always supposed to be? I sure as hell hope not, otherwise I'm going to be stuck being Confused Girl.

"Harlynn!" My mom bangs on the door, startling me. "Can I come in?"

I close my laptop and tuck my journal underneath my pillow. "Yeah." I reach over to turn the music down as she opens the door and enters my room.

Her gaze immediately drops to the clothes on the floor and the plates of half-eaten food on the dresser. "You want me to clean up for you?" she asks, glancing up at me.

She's been hovering a lot since the accident and hasn't gone back to work yet, insisting she needs to stay here and take care of me. I appreciate her concern, but I kind of just want things to go back to normal. Not that normal even exists anymore.

Maybe it never did.

Can a life return to normal after it momentarily faded into nothing?

I'm not even sure I should be here or if I was supposed to die. But someone brought me back to life.

Who are you...

"I'll clean it up in a bit." I comb my hair that desperately needs a wash out of my eyes.

She presses her lips together, glancing down at the floor again. "Are you sure? I don't mind doing it."

"It's fine." I climb off the bed and kick a few shirts out of the way. "I've just been tired, but I'll get it cleaned in a couple of days."

"Okay, if that's what you want to do." She sighs, drumming her fingers against the sides of her legs. "I want to talk to you about me going back to work. I've burnt through my sick days, and Marla's been bugging me about going back. But I don't have to if you're not ready for me to."

"You can go back to work," I tell her. "I'm perfectly fine."

"Honey, you keep saying you're fine. Always fine. And it ... it's starting to worry me."

"But I am fine." I don't think I am, though.

"You haven't even been over to see Foster yet, and he's leaving for college soon," she says quietly. "Janie said he's called you a couple of times, and you've told him you haven't felt like seeing anyone."

"Maybe I haven't," I say, scratching at the bandage on my arm.

"Then maybe you're not fine," she replies with a hint of frustration. "Dammit, I don't want to lose my patience with you, but this"—she gestures at the room—"not showering or leaving your room and ignoring Foster ... this isn't like you." She lowers her hands to her sides. "The doctor suggested we might want to set up an appointment with a therapist for you. That sometimes when people almost ... when they ... when they have near-death experiences"— she takes an uneven breath—"that it affects them mentally and can sometimes even... alter their personalities."

"Mom, I'm still the same. I've just been ... tired." *Lies, lies, lies.*

I am different. But I just can't seem to find the old Harlynn inside me, like she's still back in that lake.

"You seem ... You seem depressed."

I shake my head in denial. "I'm not depressed."

"Are you ...? Are you maybe scared that whoever hit you might try to hurt you again?"

Honestly, I hadn't thought about that until she mentioned it. But now that she has...

"Is that something the police are worried about?" I ask.

"No, not really. They think more than likely it was an accidental hit and run, but ..." Her eyes water up. "Your father and I just worry about you."

"I know you guys do." I step forward and hug her.

"I just want you to be okay," she whispers, hugging me tightly.

"I'm fine," I say.

When she starts to cry, I know I need to do something to assure her that I'm okay even if deep down I may not be.

"Before you came in here, I was actually thinking about texting Foster and telling him I want to go over there and hang out." I pull back from her arms and plaster on a fake grin. "I might even get really crazy and take a shower before I do."

She dabs her tears away with her fingertips. "I think he'd like that."

"Me showering?" I tease with a forced smile.

She gives me an unimpressed look. "No, you going to visit him. I'm sure all this has been hard on him, too."

"Yeah, I know ... Wrecking like that and remembering it ..."

"I wasn't really talking about the wreck, but I'm sure that's also been hard on him," she says. When I raise a brow, she pats my shoulder. "I think it might've been even more hard for him to see you like that and thinking he might ... lose you." Her voice catches.

I wrestle back a frown. "Oh yeah."

"You've always been so important to him." She smooths her hand over her head. "Honestly, everyone's always been a bit surprised you two haven't dated. But you're still young, so maybe that's a good thing. I have a feeling when you guys do date, it'll last forever, and I'm not ready for a wedding yet."

"Me neither," I quickly agree.

Weddings? Forever? I can't even think about that stuff right now. Not with so much unknown floating around me. Plus, I'm only eighteen.

But going over to Foster's might be a good idea still, so I can get to the bottom of the truth and feel normal again. And hell, maybe I'll luck out and he'll cave when I ask him for the truth. The Foster I thought I knew would eventually tell me. Then again, the Foster I thought I knew rarely lied to me. That's what I believed anyway.

"I'm going to text Foster, then take a shower." I pick up my phone from off the dresser to show her that I'm going to follow through with what I'm saying. That I'm fine.

"Good." Her lips tug upward as she backs out of the

room. "I'm going to call Marla and tell her I need a couple of days off."

"Mom, you can go back to work. In fact, I probably need to go back to work soon, too." Not that my boss has been bitchy about me missing days.

I work at a quaint bookstore that has a total of three employees, including my boss, and it gets maybe ten customers on a good day. I like my job, though. I love books; the smell of them, the excitement of reading them.

"I'm okay with you visiting Foster, but maybe take a few more days off work, okay?" she says. "I don't want you overdoing it."

I nod, and then she leaves the room, shutting the door behind her.

My gaze instantly drops to my phone. The screen is covered with notifications of unread messages. I've barely texted anyone since the accident, but people have been messaging me day and night. People I hardly know. I haven't responded to any of them, except for Alena and Foster.

I give a quick scroll through and decide to delete the messages from the people I don't really know. When I'm finished, there are four messages left; two from Foster, one from Alena, and strangely, one from Porter.

I open Alena's first, because hers seems like the easiest to deal with.

Alena: I'm sitting here on a balcony in Paris, and all I can think about is my crazy BFF back home. You're messing up my trip, bitch! But seriously, how are you? I wish I was there. No, eff that. I wish you were here.

Me: I'm fine. Most of my injuries are healed. And I'm actually heading over to see Foster. He's leaving this weekend, so I'm going to be stuck here all by myself.

Next, I read Foster's messages.

Foster: Hey, just wanted to check in with you again and see how you are feeling.

Foster: I know you said you're tired, but maybe I can come over for a little bit? I really miss you.

His warm lips on mine ...

Not Foster's lips ...

Sighing, I message Foster back.

Me: Actually, can I come over in a bit? I really need to get my lazy ass out of my room.

His response takes a minute or two.

Foster: You know you don't even have to ask. But, are you sure you don't want me to come over there? It might be easier for you.

Me: Nah, I need a break from my room.

And I think it might put my mom at ease if she sees me leave the house. She's been worried sick and driving me crazy.

Foster: I'm sure she's just worried about you. We all have been.

Me: I know. And I'm sorry about that.

Foster: You don't need to be sorry. You've been through a lot.

Me: So have you.

Foster: I know. And do you know what'll make me feel better?

Me: An endless amount of M&Ms and a jet ski?

Foster: No. Although, both those things sound awesome. But I was talking about you.

Me: All right. Give me about an hour to take a shower, and then I'll walk over.

Foster: I can pick you up if you want.

Me: I can walk. You only live a couple of blocks away, and I could use the fresh air.

Foster: All right. Just text me when you leave so I can keep an eye out for you.

He's acting so paranoid right now, so unlike Foster. Just how much did this accident affect him? Or is he worried about something else, like about whoever hit us?

Maybe my mom was sugarcoating the truth about our accident just being an accidental hit and run. Maybe it was an intentional hit and run. Or maybe he's just concerned about my health. Who the heck knows? Hopefully, when I see him, I can get to the truth.

The truth.

The truth.

The truth.

Does it even exist anymore?

FOURTEEN
HARLYNN

After I get done messaging Foster, I grab a pair of black shorts, a striped tank top, and a pair of clean underwear and a bra before heading into the bathroom to take a shower. It feels good to wash my hair and the grime off my skin, so I end up staying in there long enough that my mom eventually knocks on the door to see if I'm okay.

Taking the hint that it's time to get out, I shut off the water, climb out, and dry off. Then I pull on my clean clothes and take out the blow dryer so I can do my hair. Then I drag my hand across the mirror to wipe away the fog, and as my gaze collides with my reflection, an image pierces my brain.

Water all around me, drowning me and pulling the truck down. I'm sinking, sinking, sinking, and fear courses through my veins, heavy and weighing me down.

I'm going to die.

All by myself with nothing but darkness and my fear...

I blink.

I was so scared in that truck, the fear more dark and potent than even the water. I thought I was going to die. I did for a second. And then I came back. But, did I really? Am I the same Harlynn who went into the water? I look the same on the outside. Well, almost. My eyes ... they do look different. More haunted. Like they can and have seen more.

What is the truth?

Who am I now?

Who was I ever?

What did I see when I died?

I stare at my reflection until my eyes burn, until I can't see anything but blurry misshapen shapes and colors. I stare so long my eyes begin to water. I stare until my pupils ache. I stare and stare and stare, hoping I can remember something. Feel something. But *nothing* happens other than my wrist starts to itch.

I glance down at the bandage wrapped around my injured flesh. I haven't seen what's underneath it; what kind of wound is hidden there. Maybe seeing it will strike a memory.

Grabbing the edge of the bandage, I peel it back like a layer of skin from bone, unwinding, unwinding,

unwinding until it all comes off like a veil lifting from my mind.

Beneath it is dried blood and cuts; little truths that I did get hurt that night. If I stare long enough at it, it kind of looks like a feather. A feather with rough edges.

Lifting my wrist, I press my finger to the top of the injury and trace along the lines. It starts to split open like a popped stitch, weeping blood. Pain weeps through my body, along with dark red blood. Both show I am indeed alive even though I might not always feel like it.

"Harlynn, are you okay in there?" my mom asks from the other side of the shut door.

I pause. "Yeah."

"Okay...It's just that you've been in there for a while, and I'm ... I'm starting to worry."

"I'm fine," I lie.

I'm not fine. I have my finger stuck inside an injury just so I can try to remember what happened.

"Okay." My mom doesn't say anything more, but I can feel her presence outside the door, as if she's waiting for something to happen.

Sighing, I pull my finger out of my cut, and the pain slips away from me.

Then I wash my hands and the cut off, rewrap it, and start blow-drying my hair. Once it's mostly dry, I sweep it to the side in a tangled mess of waves, then dab on some lip gloss, trace my eyes with kohl eyeliner, and exit the bathroom. My mom is gone and has migrated to the kitchen, much to my relief.

I grab my phone and some cash then slip on my sandals and head for the front door.

"I'm heading to Foster's," I call out to my mom as I pass the kitchen.

She's standing by the stove, mixing something in a steaming pot, and glances up at me. "You want me to drive you? I can turn this off for a few minutes." She starts to reach for the burner knob.

I lift up my hand. "It's, like, two minutes away. I'll be fine."

She hesitantly moves her hand away from the knob. "Text me when you get there. And if it's dark by the time you come home, either call me or your father to come pick you up, or have Foster drive you, okay?"

I nod then hurry out the door before she changes her mind about driving me.

As I step outside into the fresh, summer air and sun, I breathe it in deeply, realizing how stuffy my room was becoming. Starting down the driveway, I retrieve my phone to text Foster and tell him I'm on my way. But as I tap open my messages, I get distracted by the unread text from Porter.

I should just delete it. It's not like Porter and I are

friends. The only reason I have him saved in my contacts because Star gave me his number at that party in case we got separated and I couldn't get ahold of her.

But I'm curious, so I decide to open the message.

Porter: Hey Har, I heard what happened and just wanted to make sure you're okay. If you ever need anything, you can text me.

If he hadn't used my nickname, I'd wonder if he sent the message to the wrong number because it's so... nice.

And Porter has never been nice to me.

Beyond confused, I text back a simple message.

Me: I'm okay.

Then I stuff my phone into my back pocket and turn onto the sidewalk.

The neighborhood I live in is a quiet area near the forest, with an acre of land dividing each house. Most of the homes are two-stories, except for a few, including mine. My family isn't quite as wealthy as the other families who live around here. I think the only reason my parents ever moved here was to live close to the Avertonsons, who live in one of the nicest homes in the neighborhood.

Foster's dad owns a couple of businesses in town, including the grocery store, and makes a pretty nice income. My dad works as an accountant and actually does accounting for Foster's dad's businesses, although he doesn't make nearly as much, hence the smaller house. The Avertonsons also have nicer cars, and they bought Foster a truck for his birthday and gave Kingsley his car. I was a bit surprised they gave Kingsley one, since at that point, he'd gotten in trouble a lot. Foster was surprised, too, and kind of pissed off.

"I just think it's really unfair they gave him one, too, when I work so hard to be the good son," he gripes as we sit with our feet in his pool, eating leftover birthday cake.

"Well, at least you aren't stuck driving him every- where," I try to offer a silver lining.

"Yeah, until he does something stupid and wrecks his car," he mutters then shoves a piece of cake into his mouth.

The reality, though, is Kingsley takes care of his car and has never been in an accident. Foster, technically has.

I scrunch my nose at the thought. What is wrong with me? Foster is my friend. Foster is the guy I was—am—in love with. And now I'm suddenly comparing him to Kingsley?

Shoving thoughts of Kingsley aside, I veer off my street and down a side road. I notice a blue truck with tinted windows driving just behind me. Instead of passing me, the driver slowly follows, the engine idling loudly.

I think about the person who ran into Foster's truck and how they're still out there, somewhere, maybe even aware Foster and I are okay. And for all they know, we might have seen them. What if they come after me?

As I near the corner of the next street, I dare a glance over my shoulder to check if the front end of the truck has any dents or has fragments of grey paint from Foster's truck.

It looks dent-free and sparkling clean; no evidence of a recent wreck. That doesn't mean anything, though. They could've gotten their truck fixed by now.

A heartbeat later, it drives past me and pulls into a driveway just up the street.

Breathing in relief, I turn down the street that leads to Foster's.

A few uneventful minutes later, I'm walking up to the front porch of his parents' spacious, two-story house that has a gated yard and wraparound porch. A shiny new red truck is parked in the driveway—Foster's new ride I'm guessing. The sight of it kind of irks me.

Liar, liar, liar. He lies, refuses to tell me the truth, and gets a new truck.

Blowing out an exasperated breath, I knock on the door a couple of times. When no one answers, I let myself in.

The house is quiet, except for the thrum of music playing from somewhere.

I make my way past the living room and up the stairs.

On the second floor, the music gets louder. It's not coming from Foster's room, but farther down the hallway. From Kingsley's room. His door is halfway open. Weirdly enough, the song is the same one I was listening to earlier.

I pause, eyeballing Foster's shut door then glance back at Kingsley's room. Since when does he listen to the same music as I do? Has he always, and I just never paid enough attention? Possibly. I'm usually so caught up in Foster when I'm here that I barely pay attention to much of anything else. Right now, though, my head feels Foster-free.

Pressing my lips together, I wander down the hallway toward Kingsley's room. I haven't been in there since before the day on the docks when I fell into the lake. I'm not even sure what compels me to go in there now, if the wreck took more of my sanity away than I thought.

When I reach the doorway, I peek inside. I'm not sure if I'm relieved or disappointed that he isn't in there. I should probably leave. I have no business being here. And besides, I made a promise to myself to keep my distance from him. Not that I've always held true to it.

With a glance back over my shoulder, I step inside Kingsley's room and peer around at the posters covering the black and grey walls, noting they're all bands I listen to. His room is also very dark. The blanket on his made bed is black, along with the headboard. So is the closet door and the desk. The area is cleaner than I imagined it'd be, with only a few items of clothing on the floor. His desk is neatly organized and so are the books on the shelf. What really captures my attention, though, is the collage of photos on the wall; photos of spots from around town, of random people, of the night sky, the stars, and ... Wait. Is that a photo of me?

I inch closer to get a better look. Sure enough, in the middle of the collage is a picture of me. I'm sitting on my front porch, reading a book. From the way the sun glistens across my face and with how bloomed the flowers are that line the grass around the porch, it's clearly summertime. My hair is a mess, and I'm wearing an old pair of shorts and a tank top, but I look content.

Content? Have I felt like that since the accident?

"What're you doing in here?" Kingsley's voice suddenly sails over the music.

I feel as though I should be tense—in the past I would've—but for some reason I'm not.

In fact, I'm strangely calm at the moment.

Biting on my bottom lip, I twist around to face him.

He's standing in the doorway, dressed in dark jeans, a black T-shirt, and a chain dangles from his belt loop. His normal array of leather bands covers his wrists and bruises cover his knuckles.

Beautiful. He is so beautiful.

I blink the overpowering thoughts from my mind, my gaze dropping to the bruises on his knuckles. "How did you bruise your hand?"

He eyes me over. "Why are you in my room?"

"I was ..." *You were what, Harlynn? You know you don't have an excuse, so you might as well just tell the truth.* "I heard the music. I was listening to this exact song right before I came over here, and I ... Well, honestly I wandered in here for no reason. And then I saw your photos and ..." I offer him an apologetic look. "I'm sorry. I had no right to come in here. I think I'm just tired or something." *Or something is right.*

Kingsley's intense gaze dissects me. "Are you okay? I mean, with the whole accident thing?" His gaze descends to the bandage on my wrist.

I rotate my arm over and stare at the blood-stained bandage, the fresh blood a reminder of what I did in the bathroom.

"Yeah, I'm fine. My wrist is the only thing that still hurts." *And only because I made it hurt.* "Everything else is healed. Well, except for my head. Or my memory anyway."

Healed.

I am healed.

Which means I'm not broken.

Which means I'm going to feel like this forever.

"I heard you couldn't remember much about what happened," he says, his expression guarded. "Do the doctors know why?"

I absentmindedly pick up a book from off his desk to keep from fidgeting. "Yeah, she said she thinks it's because of the emotional stress of what happened."

"That makes sense, I guess." He pauses. "How much can you remember?"

"Not much ... I can't even remember going off the cliff or being hit." I pause. "I do remember someone giving me mouth-to-mouth. That's it, though. Just lips and air and ..." *Warmth.*

He elevates his brows. "You mean you can remember *Foster* giving you mouth-to-mouth?"

I smash my lips together, rotating the book around in my hand. I'm unsure why, but I don't want to lie to him.

"You took a photo of me," I say instead of answering him, pointing at the photo on the wall.

He doesn't glance at it. "Yeah. I also took a photo of a random stranger in the park. It doesn't mean anything."

I nervously open and close the book in my hand. "I never said it did."

We stare each other down, and I'm highly aware of how he curls his fingers into fists at his sides.

He's frustrated with me and his frustration grows as he glances down at the book I'm holding.

I look down just in time to see a collage of photos—

He snatches it from me, tosses it onto his bed, and crosses his arms. "That's Porter's."

Just what exactly is in that book?

"Does it bother you that I'm in here?" I ask, watching his reaction closely.

"Why are you in here?" he questions, shifting his weight uneasily. "We're not friends. You made that pretty damn clear a long time ago."

A protest works up my throat, but I bite it back. He's right. I have made it pretty damn clear, ever since that day on the dock. But for the last few years, he's acted as if he's despised me, so ...

"So have you." The truth falls from my tongue and crashes on the floor between our feet. Shatters. It's something I've wanted to say for years—to ask him why he started loathing me. And it only took me dying and coming back to life to be able to do so. "I know you don't like me."

"I don't..." His fingers twitch at his sides. "You should probably go now."

I shake my head, pretending to be more confident than I really am. "Not until you tell me why."

His brows dip. "Why what?"

"Why you hate me."

"I don't hate you."

"You don't?" I question with doubt. "Really?"

He lifts a shoulder, appearing casual as can be. Or well, he would except his fingers are trembling. "Why would I hate you?"

I remain silent, studying him. The longer I stare, the more I feel drawn to him, like an invisible rope is woven between us, tethering me to him.

Before I know what I'm doing, I step toward him.

He quickly steps back.

I halt. "Are you afraid of me?"

He swallows shakily. "Yes."

The truth hurts. But not the same kind of pain as when I stuck my finger in my wound. This pain radiates from deep inside my chest, torturous rejection ripping at my recently healed lungs and reminding them of what it felt like to wither. I'm not even sure why it hurts so badly, to hear him say he's afraid of me.

"I didn't mean that," he quickly says when he notes my expression. "I just..." He swallows hard.

I stare at him for so long he starts to squirm. "No, you are afraid of me." My chest constricts even more. "Why?"

After spending years of convincing myself I'm afraid of Kingsley, maybe I deserve this. Deserve for him to be afraid of me when I'm no longer afraid of him. Not that I'm convinced I ever was truly afraid of him. Looking back now, when I made that vow to keep my distance from him that day, I think the basis of my decision stemmed from Foster and those words he uttered to me while we were on the shore.

"Don't tell anyone I said this, but sometimes it scares me how much he watches you."

If he had never said it, I wonder if I would've spent the last six years avoiding Kingsley. Then again, being friends with Foster has always meant being enemies with Kingsley. It used to not bother me. But it does now. Why?

Why?

Why?

Why?

He rubs his lips together. "Look, I really think you should go find my brother. I know he's been wanting to see you." When I scrunch my nose, his brows dip. "What's that look for?"

Crap. I didn't mean to do that. "I..." I shrug. "I don't know."

He chews on his bottom lip, assessing me. "Are you two fighting or something?"

"Or something," I mumble then sigh. "Sorry, I don't know what my problem is. I just feel so... different since the accident."

His gaze searches mine and then his expression softens. "I'm sure that's probably normal, considering what you've been through."

I appreciate him trying to make me feel better, but nothing about how I've been acting is normal.

"Yeah, maybe." As I stare into his eyes, I have the strangest compulsion to touch him, to run my fingers along his jawline, through his hair, across his piercings. I wonder what he'd do if I tried. Probably run the hell away. "I just feel weird. Like I didn't come back right."

They're the most truthful words I've uttered since the accident, and I can't figure out why I decided to say them to him, other than because of this strange pull I suddenly feel toward him.

Safe. I feel safe right now.

"Come back right from where?" he asks with his brows dipped.

"You heard I died for a second, right?"

He gives a cautious nod. "I assumed you did since Foster had to give you mouth-to-mouth."

I struggle not to pull a face at the mention of Foster saving me, but I'm not sure if I succeed. "Well, ever since I woke up in the hospital, I feel... I don't know... Distant. Confused. Detached." I wrap my arms around myself. "I don't feel like myself, and I've been reading these articles online about near-death experiences and I..." I blow out a breath. "I'm starting to wonder if I didn't come back the same person."

He briefly hesitates before saying, "You probably didn't."

While I pretty much said the same thing, hearing him say it is like a slap across the face.

I am not the same.

I am different.

"I didn't mean it in a bad way. I just... I think anyone who went through what you did would probably be affected by it. I'm sure eventually you'll start feeling like yourself again, but maybe not completely. I mean, what happened... It had to be..." His voice starts to crack and he quickly clears it. "Shit like that changes you, you know. But it can be in a positive way, if you want it to be."

My head angles to the side. "How so?"

He lifts a shoulder. "You could see it as a second chance to do all the things you wanted to do but were too afraid to do. Or do something good." He shrugs again. "But what the hell do I know?"

I stare at him, realizing I feel a bit better than I have since I woke up in the hospital. Who would've thought that Kingsley, the twin everyone considers the bad one, would be the one to make that happen.

"I think you might know a lot more than you give yourself credit for," I tell him with a small smile.

He smiles back at me and it's the most beautiful thing I've ever seen. It makes me feel warm inside, makes me want to keep this conversation going so I can latch onto that warmth.

"I—"

"Well, well, well, if it isn't dead girl, alive and in the flesh." Porter strolls into the room with a grin on his face.

The smile quickly vanishes from Kingsley's face.

No, don't go back to being sad. I want to see your smile again. I don't want to sink back into the cold numbness again.

Kingsley steps away from me, his frown deepening.

Dammit, Porter.

"So, you heard I died, huh?" I say flatly to Porter.

Porter's brow quirks upward. "For someone who's speaking about their own death, you sure seem uninterested."

"Am I supposed to be interested in my death?" I question with my brows raised.

"No, but you sound like a zombie right now... Wait? Are you one?" he teases. When I narrow my eyes at him, he smirks. "You know, I found your reply to my message insulting. I put the effort in to check up on you and all you can say is, *you're okay?*"

I give a half shrug. "I'm not sure what else you wanted me to say. It's not like we text each other all the time. In fact, usually I try to avoid you."

He presses his hand to his chest. "How you wound me

so, dead girl."

I narrow my eyes at him, but I'm not as offended as I'm pretending to be. His bluntness is kind of like a breath of fresh air after everyone has been so careful around me.

Careful liars.

"Stop calling me that," I tell Porter, struggling not to smile.

He shakes his head. "Nah, it's too fitting of a name."

Kingsley scowls at Porter. "Dude, stop being an asshole."

"What?" Porter shrugs innocently, his gaze wavering from me. "I'm just teasing her."

Kingsley's glare deepens. "Well, you need to stop."

Porter studies him, a slow smile curling at his lips. "Look at you, defending her. It's about damn time."

"You say that like I need defending all the time," I intervene. "But I don't."

"That's not what I was talking about." Porter is speaking to me, but staring at Kingsley, who's glaring daggers at him in return. "I'm referring to my dumbass friend finally doing what he should've done a long time ago."

"Knock it off," Kingsley snaps in a low tone.

Porter's grin broadens. "I will for now. But now that you've cracked open that door, I'm going to keep pushing on it until it opens all the way."

I glance between the two of them as they stare each other down. What on earth is he talking about?

"This coded conversation you guys are having is kind of annoying," I announce, but none of them so much as glance in my direction.

Great. Have I become invisible?

Finally, Kingsley rakes his fingers through his blond hair. "I'm done talking about this right now. We have shit to do."

Porter gives Kingsley a pressing look. "That's fine, but we're gonna circle back to it."

"No," Kingsley says in a firm, sharp tone. "We're not doing this. Not now." He snatches his car keys off the dresser. "I'm out of here. If you want to ride with me, you better drop this or I'm leaving your ass here."

Porter rolls his eyes. "Whatever. You're just avoiding the truth, like always."

The truth ...

Truth.

Truth.

Truth.

Kingsley stuffs his keys into his pocket and starts for the door without so much as a glance in my direction. And the moment we shared together before Porter interrupted us evaporates into air and blows away.

I could just let it.

It might be for the better.

But is it?

I haven't felt this calm since the accident and I want to hold onto it.

"Where are you going?" I ask Kingsley right before he walks out.

"Out," he replies without meeting my gaze.

Then he practically runs out of the room.

I give a questioning glance at Porter, but all he does is shrug then stroll after Kingsley, calling over his shoulder, "Take care of yourself, dead girl. I'm sure I'll be seeing you soon."

Then he walks out, leaving me standing alone in the bedroom.

Alone.

I feel so alone lately.

That dull ache pierces against my skull again, and I rub the heel of my hand against my forehead as I move to leave the room. But as I pass Kingsley's bed, I pause, my gaze dropping to the book I was holding earlier. He acted nervous when I started to open it, which makes me want to see what's inside it.

Chewing on my bottom lip, I try to talk myself out of doing it. It's so out of character for me. Or, well, the old me.

But I find myself opening the book anyway and fanning through the pages.

Pages and pages covered in photos, some of landscapes, some of random people, and some of me. In a few, I'm by myself. Some I'm with Foster or my family. In some of them I look content, but in some, especially the ones I'm in with Foster, I look a bit tense. Is that how I am around him? Tense? And why are there so many photos in here of me? Kingsley said this book was Porter's, but why would he keep it in his room if the book belonged to Porter?

Whether the book is Kingsley's or Porter's, I should be a bit concerned, right? After all, it seems kind of stalkerish. Although, none of the photos are creepy, just of me doing things I love, like reading, hanging out with my family and friends. Honestly, it's kind of like a map that makes up my life. Still, I have to wonder why Kingsley has this.

I think about those words Foster said to me on the shore that day, how Kingsley watches me a lot, how it's scary how much he watches me.

I agreed with him at the time, but now... I'm unsure how I feel.

I'm not really sure what I feel about anything anymore.

FIFTEEN
HARLYNN

After I leave Kingsley's room, I feel tired and even more confused than when I showed up here. I debate whether or not to just go home. I could text Foster and tell him I changed my mind about coming over. I may have done just that except when I walk past Foster's bedroom, the door swings open and he steps out.

His eyes widen when he sees me then a smile graces his lips. "Hey, I was just wondering where you were. You never texted me, so I wasn't sure if you'd left your house yet or not."

"Sorry. I forgot to send a message when I left."

Frowning, he searches my face for something. Perhaps my lies? I wonder how easy I am to read? Am I like a book with the title written on the front of me? What does the title say?

"Are you okay?" he asks. "You seem a bit off?"

"I'm fine." I put on my best fake smile. "Are you okay?"

He nods, confusion written all over his face, but he quickly shakes it off. "I'm glad you're here. I missed you." He reaches out, slips his fingers through mine, and pulls me toward him.

Pulls me right toward his lying lips.

His mouth burns against mine, scalds my tongue, and brands me with more lies.

When he draws back, a ghost of a smile is on his lips. "We really need to do that more. You seriously have the softest lips, even with the lip ring. Although, they'd be a hell of a lot softer if you'd just take that thing out."

I don't answer him, my insides twisting into thorny knots that stab beneath my flesh. The wound underneath the bandage begins to pulsate, throbbing, reminding me of that night and the days afterward. How I'm almost certain Foster lied to me.

"So, what have you got packed so far?" I change the subject, leaning to the side and peering into his room.

Scratching his forehead, he steps back into his room, gesturing for me to follow. When I step inside, he shuts the door behind me.

"I have most of my books and stuff from my shelves packed up." He points at a stack of boxes, and then at his closet. "I still need to pack my clothes and take my bed apart."

"You want me to help you with that?"

"Yeah ... sure ..." He massages the back of his neck. "Are you sure you're okay? I feel like you're mad at me or something."

"I'm not," I promise, which is the truth. I'm not sure what I'm feeling right now, other than a hell of a lot of confusion.

Story of my damn life.

"Your mom mentioned you've been spending a lot of time in your room," he says, watching me closely

"Resting, like I was instructed to do by the doctor."

"She also said you barely showered or cleaned your room."

"Are you worried about my personal hygiene?" I do my best to keep my tone light, but I'm not sure if I reach the mark or not.

He doesn't even so much as crack a smile. "No, I'm worried about you. You've been through a lot, and I ... We're all worried that maybe you're avoiding dealing with what happened."

"But, what did even happen? It's not like I know. All I know is the limited amount of information people have told me. For all I know, that could all be lies."

"I already said it's better if you don't know." His patronizing tone grates on my nerves.

Irritation rises to the surface, and it's like a zap of electricity through the sea of confusion that's been lulling inside me.

"What happened that night?" I ask. "Please just tell me."

The corners of his lips tug downward. "I can't. That night was too awful." For a fleeting moment, I swear guilt flashes across his face.

I fold my fingers inward and stab my fingernails into my palms. The pain eliminates the annoyance pulsating through me. "I can handle it."

"No, you can't. You're sweet and innocent and you sometimes still pretend that unicorns exist, and I ..." He molds his palm to my cheek. "I just don't want you to remember any of that—the fear, the pain, the terror."

"Is that really why you won't tell me? Because you think I'm innocent?" I question because it feels like there's more to it. I don't know why I feel that way. Perhaps because beneath the fog clouding my mind, I can sense the truth.

"I don't think. I know."

His words make my lips twitch.

"Have you thought that all along? That I'm innocent?"

He nods. "It's not a bad thing, though. In fact, it's one of my favorite things about you."

His warm lips on mine ...

Breathing air into my lungs ...

He thinks I'm innocent?

"I'm not as innocent as you think," I mumble, recalling the party I went to with Star. The trouble we got into. How I got my first make out session.

When he gives me a disbelieving look, the annoyance sparks as hazy memories of us kissing in his truck before it went over the cliff trickle through my mind. How his lips touched mine. How his hands roamed across my body. How he started to slip his fingers down the front of my shorts. How I wanted him to stop but couldn't get the words out. How I'm not sure if he did stop, because everything became so blurry after that.

Rage simmers underneath my skin.

I need to remember. Need to figure this out.

My mind races as I stand on my tiptoes, press my lips to his, and try to drag the truth from his lips.

Trying to breathe the lies out of his lungs and spit them out onto the floor.

He instantly deepens the kiss and cups my breast, backing me up and lying me down on the bed. Then he lines his body over mine and his hands wander all over me as his lips sear mine, filling my taste buds with bitterness and making the sea of confusion stir inside me.

"Tell me what really happened that night," I whisper as he traces his lips down to my neck while undoing the button of my shorts. "I need to know."

"Later," he whispers then slips his fingers underneath my waistband.

The anger inside me morphs to fear.

I don't want this.

I want ... Well, I'm not sure what I want, but it's not this. I just kissed him because I felt so frustrated and confused and it's making me feel as if I'm losing my damn mind.

"Foster?" Janie calls out, knocking on Foster's bedroom door.

"Fuck." He quickly pushes off me and ruffles his hair back into place. Then his gaze shifts to me, to my undone shorts. "You should probably do your button up or else she's going to give us a safe sex lecture," he teases with a smile.

Sitting up, I slowly do up the button, trying to hide how shaky I feel inside and not in a good way.

He places a quick kiss on my lips. "I love you. And I'm so glad you're here with me." Then he gets up from the bed to answer the door.

I lift my hand to my lips and roughly rub them, trying

to rub off the lies he fed me and the feel of his lips that I'm now positive weren't the ones that breathed life into me that night.

"Hey," Janie says when Foster opens the door. "Your dad and I need to talk to you for a second ..." Her gaze travels to me and a smile appears on her lips. "Harlynn, I didn't know you were here. I'm so glad you finally decided to come over."

"Me, too." My smile is all plastic.

She smiles then looks at Foster. "Can you come into your dad's office for a moment? He needs to talk to you about a couple of things about this weekend."

"Sure." Foster moves to leave, throwing me a smile from over his shoulder. "I'll be right back. Don't go anywhere, okay?" He doesn't wait for me to respond, simply leaves, as if he expects me to be here when he gets back.

But I guess, in the past, I always was. Just waiting around for him.

"It's really nice to see you," Janie says to me. "And can you tell your mom when you see her that we're definitely on for Sunday?"

"Sure." I keep on smiling until she leaves then let my smile fizzle as I flop down on the bed.

I can feel everywhere Foster touched me, as if his palms seared away my flesh. I shouldn't have allowed him to touch me. I'm not even sure why I did. Just like I'm not sure why I'm here, just waiting around for him to come back and feed me more lies.

As I'm staring at the wall, trying to decipher if I have any feelings left in me for Foster other than frustration, I decide it's time to leave. Standing up, I cross the room, feeling a bit shaky and I end up bumping into a stack of boxes and books spill out all over the floor.

"Shit." I start to pick them up when something shiny and silver falls out of one of them.

When I pick it up, my heart slams against my chest.

My fucking necklace.

How long has Foster had this? Since I lost it all those years ago? Why did he keep it?

Gritting my teeth, I stuff the necklace into my pocket, storm out of the room, down the stairs, and out of the house, preparing to head home. But I pause the second I step onto the porch as I hear voices floating over from the driveway.

"You're going to have to tell her the truth eventually." Porter says.

It's late, the stars and moon are gleaming in the sky and the porch light isn't on, so it's dark enough that I can't see them.

"Listen," I swear the wind whispers.

I tense and nearly run back into the house, but then I

find myself curious enough to hunker down in the shadows and listen.

Yeah, apparently on top of becoming a thief, an emotionless shell, and maybe even crazy, I've now become an eavesdropper too.

"You know I can't tell her." Kingsley sounds stressed. "It's too risky. Plus, it's not like she'd believe me anyway."

"She might," Porter replies. "I mean, she was in your room for hell's sake, and you two were grinning at each other like a couple of lovestruck idiots when I walked in. There's no way she could still be afraid of you."

"We weren't grinning like lovestruck idiots. We were just... Talking. And I'm not even sure why she was in my room. She was just in there when I walked in." Kingsley gives a short pause. "She does seem less afraid of me, though. And I think she's mad at Foster for some reason."

Porter snorts a laugh. "For some reason? Because I can think of about twenty reasons off the top of my head that gives her every right to be pissed at your asshole of a brother."

"Maybe, but Harlynn is... in love with that asshole of a brother you're referring to," Kingsley utters. "She has been since we were kids. And if she's mad at him right now, she'll eventually get over it. She always does."

"Maybe not after this," Porter says. "I mean, this is big, you know."

"Yeah, I know, but still..."

"Still nothing. You don't know what's going to happen, so stop assuming you do." Porter pauses. "But she might end up pissed off at you too the longer you keep the truth from her."

Kingsley sighs. "I know, but like I said, it's too risky. I mean, if anyone else found out..."

"You could always just ask her to keep it a secret."

"Maybe."

They grow quiet after that. Car doors slam, then the roar of Kingsley's car revving up fills up the quietness.

Moments later, headlights cascade across the porch as the GTO backs up onto the road. I crouch lower to avoid being seen and stay in the shadows until the car is gone.

Then I hurry off the porch toward my house, my mind filled with questions of what they could've meant by all that stuff they just said. Kingsley needs to tell me the truth? What truth?

Wait... Does he know Foster didn't save me that night? Does he know the truth about what happened? How, though?

Dammit. Why does it feel like everyone around me is lying to me?

I need to remember. Somehow.

I strain my mind to see further into that night, but a wall of darkness slams down. I try again, over and over again, so lost in my thoughts that I barely notice a person leaning against a street post just a ways up the road.

They're wearing a hoodie pulled so low I can barely see their face, but I can tell they're extremely tall—like almost inhumanly tall. "Why are you walking around alone so late at night?" His voice sounds strangely low and croaky.

Ignoring him, I pick up my pace.

He pushes away from the street post and crosses the street toward me. I walk quicker, aware of the slightest spike in my pulse, a reminder that I'm alive, even if it feels like I'm not most of the time.

"Hey, I'm not going to hurt you," he calls out as he nears the sidewalk.

I break into a run, cutting across front lawns and hauling ass for my house while digging out my phone from my pocket. I can hear him shout something after me, but I ignore him and start to dial my mom's number.

But then it suddenly grows quiet. When I glance over my shoulder, he's gone.

Still, I keep running, not slowing down until I reach my house. I barrel inside, shutting the door and locking it. Then I work to catch my breath. *Air in. Air out.*

Come on; breathe.

"Harlynn? Is that you?" My mom steps out of the

kitchen. She frowns when she sees me. "Did Foster drive you home?"

I shake my head. "No. I walked."

Her frown deepens. "I thought I told you to get a ride home if it was dark."

"Sorry. I forgot." My mind is racing so swiftly that I struggle to concentrate on what she's saying.

"You forgot?" She shakes her head in annoyance. "There was a reason I told you to get a ride. It's not safe to be walking around alone, especially at night. Not until we're absolutely certain why Foster's truck was crashed into."

"I know. And I'm sorry." I take a deep breath to steady my breathing. "Mom, I don't want you to panic, but I feel like I should probably tell you about a sketchy guy I just ran into."

Her eyes widen then she pulls out her phone from her pocket.

"What're you doing?" I ask, trailing after her as she walks toward the living room.

"Calling the detective and telling her what you just told me."

"Is that necessary?"

She nods, putting the phone up to her ear. "She told me to inform her of anything out of the ordinary or alarming— Hi, Detective," she says into the phone. "I need to report an incident that happened tonight with Harlynn."

I start to walk away, but she snaps her fingers at me, indicating for me to wait.

"I'm going to need you to give me a description of the guy," she whispers, covering the phone with her hand.

I move back toward her and tell her what I can recall about the guy. But since I didn't see he face very well, I'm not much help. I do tell her he was tall, though. So tall it was almost like he was standing on stilts. She looks at me strangely when I say that, like she was concerned maybe I hallucinated the incident.

And at this point I have to question if perhaps she's right.

Maybe this is all just one big hallucination.

SIXTEEN
HARLYNN

After I tell my mom everything I can remember about the guy, I head to my bedroom. I change into my pajamas and climb into bed, then examine the necklace I found in Foster's room, spinning the locket around, watching it spin around and around and reflect against the light.

I'm not sure why he kept this after all these years and never gave it back or how he ever found it to begin with, but I need to find out. I need to find out a lot of things about Foster.

Fastening the necklace around my neck, I pick up my phone as it vibrates. It's gone off a handful of times since I left Foster's house, and I know who the messages are from without looking.

I almost don't open them. Just let them sit unread on

my phone. Pretend he was never texting me. That he didn't lie to me. That he didn't have my missing necklace tucked into one of his books.

Pretend.

Pretend.

Pretend.

But I honestly don't feel like pretending right now.

I want things to be real again.

I want the truth.

I want to feel like myself, whoever that is now.

What I really want is to feel that warmth I briefly tasted when Kingsley smiled at me.

Swiping my finger across the screen, I open the messages.

Foster: Where are you?

Foster: Why did you leave?

Foster: I just called your mom and she said you made it home okay, but I'm still confused why you left without saying anything. Did I upset you?

Foster: Please just talk to me.

That's the last message he sends, but an unread one still remains. A message from Porter.

Porter: If you ever feel like hanging out and having some fun, text me. I know you're tech-

nically not supposed to hang out with Kingsley and if he knew I was texting you, he'd freak out. But you seemed different tonight. More talkative and less under the influence of Foster. Plus, you looked like you could use some fun.

Do I?

Lying down on my bed, I rest my hand on the locket.

The coldness of the metal against my palm is a reminder of the lie.

That Foster lied to me about having the necklace.

That he lied about saving me.

It makes me wonder what else he's been lying about.

It makes me question everything that has to do with him, which unfortunately, since he's had so much to do with my life, forces me to question everything.

WATER ALL AROUND ME, *pushing me down as metal crunches around me, cutting my flesh.*

I'm drowning.

I'm dying.

I can't breathe.

I reach out, opening my eyes and trying to see or feel

something, anything besides darkness. I feel something brush my fingers and turn my head, straining to see.

A face appears beside me, a smile painting their lips. I reach for them, begging them to help me, but they start to slip away, swimming away from me, and I sink toward the bottom of the lake, the metal crunching around me and turning into my tomb.

I am dead.

I am not Harlynn.

I am Paige—

My eyes pop open, and I frantically glance around at the purple and black walls of my bedroom, half-expecting water to be seeping out of the cracks.

"Harlynn." My mom walks into my room. She takes one look at me and presses her hand to her chest. "Thank God you're here."

I sit up, feeling a bit groggy. *What was that dream?* "Why wouldn't I be here?"

"I don't know, but I was worried about you, and I ... I'm just glad you're here."

By the look on her face, I can tell she's keeping something from me.

"Mom, please just tell me the truth," I say, rubbing my eyes. "Because I can tell you're keeping something from me."

She sighs, crosses the room, and sits down on the edge

of my bed. "I guess I should probably tell you since you're going to find out anyway... There was an incident this morning up at the lake. A couple of fishermen found a girl ..." Her voice cracks. "It looks like she's been dead for a while."

A girl dead in the lake.

A girl drowning in the lake.

Just like my dream.

"Do they know how she died?" I ask, worry pouring through my veins.

"All I've heard so far is that her car was also found in the lake, so more than likely she crashed into it and drowned."

I sink toward the bottom of the lake, the metal crunching around me and turning into my tomb.

I am dead.

I am not Harlynn.

I place my hand over my bandaged wrist as blood begins to seep through the bandage. The wound has somehow opened, the pain spreading up my arm and wiping out any fear that might be inside me. "What was her name?"

"Paige Meriforter," she says. "She's that girl who disappeared over a year ago. I don't know if you remember her or not."

I do. God, do I.

This is so weird. Why did I just dream about Paige moments before my mom came in to tell me this? Is it just a weird coincidence because I saw her flyer on the wall of the police station the other day?

"I'm so sorry, sweetie. I shouldn't be telling you any of this. This is the last thing you need to be worrying about. I just ... When I heard the news, I was thrown back to the night Foster's truck went into the ..." She releases an uneven exhale. "I didn't even realize you hadn't come home that night. Janie was the one who told me about the accident ... And then I ran in here and your bed was empty ..." She wraps her arms around me. "I'm so glad you're okay."

I hug her back, hating that she's so upset, but I'm distracted by why I dreamt about Paige last night. How she was in the water. I also can't help but think about the time in the police station when I wandered over to the flyers on the wall. How I was drawn to Paige's. How I thought I heard someone telling me to go over and look at the wall.

"Do the police know what happened to Paige?" My tone shakes a bit as my pulse increases.

She pulls back and looks at me. "Not yet, but I'm sure it was an accident. That road around that lake is danger- ous, especially at night." She sighs heavily. "There's prob- ably one more thing I need to tell you since this town loves to gossip. It's about a girl that was reported missing this morning. She's about your age too so you might know her."

Fear courses through me. "Who was she?"

"I think her name was Beth Trelarallie," she says. "Do you know her?"

Beth Trelarallie. The girl I saw Foster flirting with at the gas station the night of the accident.

I give a shaky nod. "Not well, but I do know her... But how do you know she's missing?"

"Because Miss Belfertoer loves to gossip. From what she told me, Beth was at a party when she disappeared. There's been speculation that her drink might have been drugged beforehand, but that might be the gossip mill spinning things out of control. You know how this town can be." She forces a smile. "But let's not talk about this anymore, okay? You're supposed to be taking it easy." She rises to her feet, but then pauses. "I think it'd be for the best if, at least for a while, you avoided wandering around alone. And maybe you should avoid going to parties for a bit."

I nod, my mind spinning.

Beth was drugged.

Drugged like a girl was at the last party I went to. A party I went to the night of the accident. The night I can barely remember anything about.

Drugged.

Blurry.

Hands touching me.

Lips on mine.

I can't breathe.

I blink from the distorted images.

Was I drugged that night? Is that why I can't remember much of what happened?

But I can remember up until about when Foster and I arrived at Hallows Hill, so when could I have been drugged? It's not like we were drinking in his truck. Maybe it happened at the party we were at earlier? But does it take that long for drugs to kick in?

"I'm going to go make you some French toast," my mom says. "How does that sound?"

"Good." I scoot to the edge of the bed as she exits the room.

Then I get up, shut the door, and return to my bed, mulling over what she just told me.

Beth is missing. Another girl is missing in this town.

And then there's Paige's body being found in the lake only hours after I dreamt of her death.

Nothing makes sense anymore, yet I feel like in the midst of my confusion, something is crying out to me, begging me to see the truth.

Sighing, I grab my computer and get comfortable in

my bed. Then I spend the next several hours sitting around, skim-reading articles on the internet and attempting to put together the pieces of what's going on with my mind. But the more I read, the more confused I get. Nothing makes sense anymore.

Nothing has become my middle name.

I am a hollowed shell of flesh and bones with nothing inside me. Or maybe the answers are written somewhere underneath my skin, like the wound on my wrist. Perhaps, if I peel my flesh back and look inside, I'll get the answers.

I scratch my bandaged wrist with the strongest compulsion to stab my fingernails into the wound again. This time, I'll keep digging until the truth bleeds out of me, the secrets of that night, and why I am the way I am now.

Or maybe I'll just end up bleeding to death. Who the hell knows.

Finally, after hours of staring at the computer screen, I start to grow tired. I fight off the sleepiness for a while because I'm seriously starting to hate closing my eyes, but eventually it gets the best of me and darkness pulls me under.

SEVENTEEN
HARLYNN

I'm standing in a dark closet, and music is pulsating from the other side. I'm not alone. There's a guy in here with me. I'm not sure who he is since I was blind-folded when I came in here. All I know is that I'm supposed to be kissing him. Instead, I'm standing here awkwardly, listening to the sounds of his breaths.

This was such a bad idea. Coming to this party was such a bad idea. Agreeing to play this stupid game of truth or dare was a bad idea. And maybe drinking those shots of vodka in the car was a bad idea, too.

My heart slams against my chest, my breaths leaving me in deafeningly loud gasps. I'm beyond nervous, and it's more than evident.

Maybe I should just open the door and declare that I'm a big loser. It's not like I know anyone here except Star.

Well, and Porter and Kingsley, but I haven't seen them since we arrived ...

Whoever is in here with me unexpectedly takes my hand and gives it a comforting squeeze. The gesture makes a bit of relief trickle through me.

Perhaps they're equally as nervous as I am. Although, most of the people at the party don't really seem like the type to get nervous about kissing a total stranger. Then again, everyone here seems either buzzed or high, which I find odd since no one was allowed to bring alcohol or drugs to the party. But Star and I did shots of vodka before we came in, so ...

The hand on mine slowly starts to travel upward along my arm, the palm rough and warm against my skin. When it reaches the curve of my shoulder, it slips around to the back of my neck, fingers splaying across my flesh.

My pulse quickens in a nervously excited way. I've never really been kissed before, and while I always wanted Foster to be my first real kiss, I find myself strangely excited about this. Then again, this guy could be anyone. He could be a total creeper. Yet, for some bizarre reason, I feel content. Nervously excited yet content.

"Who are you?" I whisper, even though I was told not to speak when I came in here. That was a rule Star had set when I chose dare, and she dared me to go into the closet and let her pick someone for me to make out with. I'm not *supposed to see them or say anything to them. I'm not supposed to know who I'm about to kiss.*

Their fingers tense against the back of my neck. Heavy breathing fills the space, and the sound mixes with my own rapid breathing. Then they lace their fingers through my free hand, holding on tightly as warm breaths caress the side of my face.

Oh, my word, this is really happening—

Lips brush mine, tentative at first, as if they're not really sure about this. Or maybe they're just being careful with me, as if they can sense this is my first real kiss.

Jesus, am I that transparent?

Their fingers on the back of my neck softly trace circles across my skin. The feeling is relaxing, and my eyelids start to drift shut when they suddenly part my lips with their tongue.

I gasp then cringe at the noise, my cheeks warming in embarrassment. But, as they deepen the kiss, the warmth leaves my face and travels through my body, my pulse pounding as I clutch onto their hand.

When their tongue tangles with mine, my legs tremble, and I damn near about fall down. As if sensing where my thoughts are, they shift the hand on my neck to my waist and grasp onto me, holding me steady and kissing me so deeply that I forget how to breathe.

Maybe I don't even need air at all anymore.

Warm lips on mine ...

Breathing air into my lungs ...

Breathing life into me ...

Warm lips ...

I know those lips ...

They brand me—

My eyelids fly open, and my fingers drift to my lips. Holy shit. Those lips that kissed me that night in the closet are the same ones that breathed life into me. That's why they were familiar. But I have no clue who kissed me that night, so this revelation doesn't help me get to the bottom of the mystery surrounding the night I died.

However, it's a start. And there's one person who knows who was in that closet with me. Star. She could be the key to helping me solve who saved my life. That is, if I can find her.

I haven't seen her since she dropped out of school not too long after the party. But I know some people who still hang out with her. People that I'm not sure I trust, but I may have to look past that for now.

Lowering my hand from my lips, I roll to my side and reach for my phone to check what time it is. Just after nine o'clock in the evening. It's late and my mom will have a fit if I try to leave the house. But I think this might be worth facing her wrath later if she catches me sneaking out.

Rubbing my eyes, I sit up and open the message

thread with Porter, ignoring the new messages from Foster.

Me: I want to have some fun. Can I hang out with you guys tonight?

What I really want is to talk to them about what I overheard them discussing the other night, and to try to find Star so I can ask her who kissed me in the closet. But I keep all of that to myself for now. I just hope Porter wasn't messing with me when he invited me to hang out with him, but it does kind of seem like something he'd do.

So I'll admit, I'm kind of surprised when I receive a message from him only moments later.

Porter: All right, dead girl. Fun is on the way.

EIGHTEEN
KINGSLEY

"Why the hell are we heading toward my house?" I ask Porter as he turns off the highway and into my neighborhood.

"We're not going to your house," he replies evasively. But the amused smile that rises across his face lets me know that he's about to do something that'll annoy me.

He's been my best friend since ninth grade, and while we have a lot in common, like our love for tattoos and piercings and the fact that both our parents see us as disappointments, we're also very different, like with our personalities, how we see the world, and what we find funny. And I've learned over the years that generally, when Porter smiles in amusement, I'm about to get annoyed.

"Then, why the heck are we heading into my neighborhood?" I ask as he makes a turn onto a side road that's pretty damn close to my house. "I thought we were going to the party at Dan's tonight? We're supposed to."

"We are," he assures me as he makes a circle around the same block. "This is just a quick detour."

"What kind of a detour?" I ask suspiciously.

He glances around at the sidewalk lit up by lamp-posts. It's just after ten o'clock, the neighborhood is quiet, and most of the lights in the houses are off. That's usually how it is around here, even on weekends. If you go farther south in town, though, the night comes alive, people covering the sidewalks and loitering on street corners. Night is what people should be afraid of everywhere, though.

Night is when the bad come alive.

As Porter continues to make yet another loop around the block without explaining what he's doing, my frustration builds.

"Dude, seriously, what the hell are you doing?"

"Will you chill the hell out?" He parks near a street corner, digs his phone out of his pocket, and sends a text. "This'll only take a second."

"Okay, but what are we even doing here?" I say, highly aware that we're parked on the corner of the street that leads to Harlynn's house.

I look at Porter then frown.

His gaze is locked on Harlynn's house.

Fuck. This isn't good.

"Please tell me you didn't do something stupid."

"I didn't," he promises.

That doesn't mean anything since mine and Porter's definition of stupid greatly varies.

"Porter ..." I start, but he hops out of the car before I can finish.

As he jogs across the street, heading in the direction of Harlynn's house, I grab his keys, climb out of the car, and hurry after him, making sure to stay in the shadows. If anyone sees me sneaking around, they'll probably call the cops on my ass. I'm not trusted in this town and have a bad reputation based on some lies and some truths. Not that I care. Well, most of the time I don't. I've gotten used to it at this point, used to being the sprouted weed in my family. But there are a few people's opinions that matter to me. And one of those people lives in the house I'm jogging up to.

When Porter reaches the side of the house where Harlynn's window is, he crouches down just below it. Since he's wearing all black clothing, he blends in with the shadows.

"What're you doing?" I hiss as I hunker down beside him then glance up at Harlynn's window.

Her house is only one story, which means, if she so much as glances outside, she'll probably spot us.

Grinning, Porter puts his fingers to his lips and shushes me.

I give him a cold stare and whisper, "If you don't tell me what's going on right now, I'm going to go back to your car, drive away, and leave your ass here."

"And how are you going to do that?" Grinning, he pats his pockets. "You don't have the keys ..." He frowns. "Fuck, I think I left them in the car."

"You did." I dangle them in front of his face. "And I grabbed them."

He reaches for the keys, but I quickly move my hand out of his reach.

"Tell me why we're hiding beneath Harlynn's window and I'll give them back to you. And please don't say it's about me telling her the truth. Because I'm not ready to do that yet." I don't know if I'll ever be.

I couldn't even imagine telling her what I know. She'd probably think I was insane.

He rests his hands against the ground to keep his balance. "It's ..."

The window above us suddenly slides open.

I tense, preparing to run, knowing if Harlynn sees me out here, she'll probably think I'm stalking her. It's the kind of shit Foster has been putting in her head—that I stalk her. And finding me here will be like confirming the bullshit lies he's been telling her for years now. And that little moment we had in my bedroom the other day, where she looked at me without fear, will slip away from me.

Then again, I really doubt it matters. Not after she finds out the truth. Not after she finds out that not only did my brother lie to her, but so did I. I didn't have a choice, though. I have to keep what happened a secret for several reasons, one being I'm not sure she could handle the truth.

"Hey." Harlynn pops her head out the window and looks down at us, not an ounce of surprise in her, as if she expected us to be here. She glances at Porter. "I told you I didn't need you to come up to the window. I could've walked the fifty feet by myself."

"The fact that you actually believe that shows how naïve you are," he replies with a grin.

I shake my head. For years, Porter has loved getting underneath Harlynn's skin. Not that I can blame him. The feisty side of her that comes out whenever he does is sexy as hell, and if she weren't scared of me most of the time, I'd probably seek every opportunity I could to do the same thing. But I know she's always afraid of me. Well, almost always. There have been a few occasions when she's seen past what everyone else sees in me, like yesterday when she actually smiled at me. And it was the most goddamn gorgeous thing I've ever seen.

She narrows her eyes at Porter. "I'm not naïve, asshole. I know self-defense. If you don't believe me, though, I can give you a demonstration. My favorite move is the old kick in the balls."

"Kinky. I like it." Porter grins at her, but then he sneaks me a sidelong glance, causing Harlynn to look my way.

Her big eyes that are beyond gorgeous widen for a moment but she promptly collects herself. "I didn't know you were going to come with this asshole." She points at Porter. "I guess I probably should've, though, since you two are attached at the hip." A playful smile touches her lips.

That's the thing about Harlynn and maybe where part of my fixation with her stems from. Even though she sometimes is afraid of me—and who can blame her with how I act sometimes—she always speaks directly to me while most people talk around me or pretend I don't exist, my parents being one of these people. She's even touched me a few times, and when we were younger, she hugged me. Even though it made me uncomfortable, I appreciated it—the brief human connection, the contact, the reminder that not everyone in this world hates me.

"We're not attached at the hip," I say. "And I wasn't

even aware we were coming to your house until about thirty seconds ago. If I did, we never would've shown up." Fuck, I sound like an asshole. But I'm nervous and my social skills suck, especially around her.

"Oh." She frowns, studying me with her head angled to the side, strands of her long, wavy brown hair falling into her face.

I try not to stare, but it's complicated.

If only she weren't gorgeous. And quiet, yet snarky. If only she hadn't hugged me all those years ago, giving me the very first hug I can ever remember having.

Maybe if all those things weren't true, I could get over this infatuation I have with her. Unfortunately, no matter how hard I try, I can't. Even her flaws draw me in.

Everything about her draws me in.

"Why are you looking at me like that?" she wonders, biting her bottom lip.

"Looking at you like what?" I play dumb, trying to tear my gaze off of her, but fail epically.

Shit, this is bad. I shouldn't be here tonight. Not with all the lies between us. It's dangerous if she finds out the truth and it'll ruin everything I've worked for. Plus, she's too good to be hanging out with me.

Too good.

I'm bad.

The bad one.

I've been told this forever, so much so that it's branded into my mind like invisible scars.

The bad twin.

The bad seed.

Bad.

Bad.

Evil.

That word has even been thought a few times.

I straighten my legs, no longer caring if I get caught being here.

"You know what? Never mind. It doesn't matter." I turn to leave, saying to Porter, "I'm tired of your crap. I'm heading to the party. If you're not in the car in one minute, I'm leaving your ass here." I don't look back to see if he follows me, to see what he does with Harlynn.

I don't care.

About anything.

At least, that's what I try to tell myself.

But would be the point of convincing myself of anything else? Harlynn has always belonged to my brother. That has been made clear since the day Foster decided he wanted to be friends with her.

Because my brother has—and always will—get whatever he wants.

NINETEEN
HARLYNN

I feel a bit bad for sneaking out of the house, but not enough to not do it. Even before I died and came back to life, I occasionally snuck out. But now, if my mom finds out I'm not in my room, she'll be completely freaked out. But I'm eighteen and can technically do whatever I want. And getting to the truth about what happened to me the night of the accident is more important to me now than anything else. What kind of person that makes me, who the hell knows.

"Where are we going?" I ask Porter as I follow him across the grass and toward his car parked a ways down the street.

Kingsley already made it to the car. He's also made it clear he's not happy I'm going with them. I'm not sure why, why I'm bothering him so much. Maybe I should go back to my room since clearly he doesn't want me around. But my need for answers keeps my feet moving forward.

Porter slows to a stop as he reaches his car. "To a party at Dan's cabin."

"Who's Dan?" I ask, stopping beside him.

"A friend of mine and Kings's." He opens the door and moves to lift the seat, but pauses. "You want to sit in the front?" he asks me. "There's room for all three of us."

I glance at Kingsley. He's glaring at me from the passenger seat. Part of me wants to say yes just to see how he'll react. But I decide against it. "Nah, I can sit in the back."

Shrugging, Porter flips the seat forward and lets me in. Then he climbs into the driver's seat, shuts the door, and starts up the engine.

"Put your seatbelt on," Kingsley mutters.

I assume he's speaking to Porter, but Porter chooses to ignore him, turning the car around and driving toward the highway.

Kingsley tilts his head toward me, strands of his blonde hair falling across his forehead. "Put your seatbelt on."

So he was talking to me.

"Why?" I decide to play around with him. I'm not even sure why I do it, other than I'm hoping maybe he'll chill out, and we can go back to that moment in his bedroom when I felt safe and calm.

The muscles in his jaw pulsate. "You were just in a car accident, so you should understand the importance of wearing a seatbelt."

He has a point and I plan on buckling up, but...

"I'll put mine on when you put yours on," I hold his gaze even as it becomes so intense I can barely breathe.

Kingsley's eyes darken. "There are people in this world who care about you, so do them a favor and put your damn seatbelt on."

"There's people that care about you too."

He laughs hollowly. "No one gives a shit about what happens to me."

"That's not true." But as I say it, the words feel shaky and heavy.

All the years I've been around Kingsley and watched him from afar, I've never witnessed his parent's show anything but disdain toward him. He hasn't had any close friends besides Porter and as far as I know, no girlfriends. And then there's Foster. He might be the worst when it comes to showing Kingsley how unwanted he is. And me? I'm no better.

How could I not see this before? Because I was around Foster all the time? Because I was around his words of hatred toward Kingsley, and I allowed it to poison my mind. But now I can see the truth. That Foster is a liar. Kingsley might be one too, though, but for some reason, I feel his lies are different. That the secrets he's hiding might not hurt me as much as Foster's have and will. I don't know why, why I all of a sudden feel this connection to Kingsley, but I can't seem to get rid of it and honestly, I'm not sure I want to.

"I care about you." The words are soft, but true.

Porter gives me a funny look from over his shoulder, but he surprisingly doesn't say anything.

Kingsley shakes his head with his jaw set tight. "Just put your damn seatbelt on."

Letting out a shaky exhale, I scoot forward and utter words that may get me laughed at, but I don't care at the moment. "I mean it. I care about whether or not you're safe, so come on. Lets both put our seatbelts on so we can both be safe."

He grits his teeth. "Stop messing around and just put on your seatbelt."

I slide back in the seat, getting comfortable and refusing to buckle up until he does.

"Har," he warns in a cold tone. "I mean it. Buckle up."

"Kings," I mimic his tone. "I mean it to. Buckle up."

Porter snorts a laugh. "Fuck, this might be the most entertaining thing I've ever seen."

Kingsley's gaze cuts to Porter. "Shut the hell up."

"No, thanks." Porter reaches for his seatbelt. "I, however, am going to be a good example and put my seatbelt on."

I lift a brow at Kingsley, like *well?*

He stares at me intensely, and my heart races, but I'm not afraid.

Safe.

Safe.

Safe.

Grinding his teeth, he draws his seatbelt over his shoulder and buckles up. "There? Are you happy?"

"Yeah, I am," I say as I fasten my own seatbelt.

Man, that was a lot of work, but at least I got him to do it.

Kingsley's brows pull together. "Why are you acting like this?" he asks me.

Confusion swirls through me. "Acting like what?"

"Like..." He yanks his fingers through his hair as he releases a stressed breath. "You've barely talked to me in years and usually when you do, you act like you don't want to be around me. And I know Foster tells you not to hang out with me, so why are you here, telling me to buckle up my seatbelt because you care about me?" His hand falls to his lap. "I know it's not true, so what're you up to?"

Hurt and annoyance stab at my chest. "What the heck

would I be up to?"

He gives a shrug. "I have no idea, but this... you being here... It's fucking weird and..." He shakes his head. "Does Foster know where you are?"

"No," I grumble. "And why does it matter if he does or not?"

"And are you going to tell him who you hung out with tonight?" he questions, ignoring my question.

I shrug. "Sure."

Kingsley arches a brow. "Like you told him about the last party you went to with us?"

He has a point. At the time, I told myself I didn't tell Foster about the party because he didn't need to know everything I did. But in reality, I didn't want him knowing I ditched him to go to a wild party with Kingsley, Porter, and Star. I was even a bit ashamed that I went.

Now I feel ashamed for making so many of my decisions based on what Foster thinks. A guy who I believed was my best friend, but apparently has been lying to me since our friendship first began—the necklace pressing against the hollow of my neck proves that.

"I may have not told him about going to that party," I say. "But like I told you the other day, I feel different now. And you were pretty understanding about it then."

"Is that why you wanted to come with us tonight?" he

asks. "Because you're trying new things and embracing this different side of you?"

"Kind of." It's partially the truth.

Kingsley offers me a small, but beautiful smile, and that warmth returns inside my body, making a smile touch my lips.

"I'm sorry... for being an asshole," he says. "I'm just..." He looks away from me.

Porter throws me a smile in the rearview mirror, as if we're exchanging a secret.

I frown, beyond confused, which only makes his smile broaden.

"You're so weird," I say, causing Kingsley to glance at us.

"Like you're not," Porter quips with a smirk.

Okay, he has me there.

"What're you doing?" Kingsley asks Porter, eyeing him over suspiciously.

"Nothing." But Porter's grin suggests otherwise.

Kingsley shakes his head, his irritation resurfacing.

Now that I've seen him smile a few times, I don't want to see him frown, so I decide to try to distract him from his irritation. Not that I think it's going to be easy, but I want to win him over. Want to find out more about him. Want to find out the truths he's hiding inside him.

"So, quick question." I slide forward and cross my

arms on the back of the seat. "Who's all going to be at this party? And what exactly are we going to do there?"

Porter snickers. "We're going to party, obviously, and people are going to be there." His lips tug into a smirk. "And didn't you just try to convince me you weren't naïve?"

I roll my eyes. "But seriously, who's all going to be there?" I attempt to appear and sound casual. "Is Star going to be there?"

Porter shrugs, flipping on his blinker. "She might be."

I open my mouth to ask him more questions, but he holds up a finger.

"Hold that thought." He steers into the parking lot of the gas station Foster and I were at the night of the accident.

Memories dance through my mind. Everything seemed normal while we were here.

Didn't it?

Looking back, Foster had been acting a bit weird, and Beth had been crying when I came into the store after Foster lost his wallet.

Did something happen between them?

"You should just learn to ignore Porter," Kingsley says to me, eliciting a glare from Porter. "He gets off on pissing people off."

"I figured that out a long time ago," I assure Kingsley.

Kingsley smiles at me and again, I'm reminded of how foreign the look is—how over the years, he's rarely looked happy.

"You know, I'd be super irritated about the shit you guys are saying about me, but Kings is smiling so I'm gonna let it slide." Porter tosses Kingsley a smirk as he parks in front of a gas pump.

I expect Kingsley to frown but instead he mirrors Porter's smirk. "Slide how exactly? What would you do to us if you didn't let it slide?"

Porter grins wickedly. "Kick your asses."

Kingsley crooks a brow. "So you're saying you'd kick Harlynn's ass too?"

Porter's eyes glint deviously. "Even if I tried, you'd never let me get within ten feet of her, isn't that right?"

Kingsley's mood goes *poof*. "Shut up, man."

Porter disregards him, flicking a glance in my direction as he shuts off the engine. "Hey Har, did you know you have your very own protector—"

Kingsley smacks Porter's arm, kind of hard.

"Fuck," Porter gripes, gripping his arm. "That hurt."

"Good," Kingsley says without a drop of remorse.

Shaking his head, Porter shoves open the door. "I'm going to fill up. Go get me a soda and some of those chips I had the other night." He doesn't wait for Kingsley to respond, climbing out and shutting the door.

"What do I look like, his little bitch or something?" Kingsley mutters, massaging his temples with his fingertips.

I watch him, questions cramming my mind. "He seems to think so."

He lowers his hands and turns his head toward the window. Silence stretches between us as he stares out at the mostly vacant gas station, and I can't help but wonder what he's thinking.

Just who is Kingsley? While I've known him all my life, I feel like I barely know anything about him. And I want to know him now, want to know what causes the sadness that almost always haunts his eyes.

"I don't want to sound like a jerk, but what's the full reason you're here? Because it feels like there's more than what you're telling us," he says, startling me a bit.

"Why does it bother you that I'm here?" I answer his question with a question to avoid telling him the real reason.

His gaze collides with mine. "It doesn't bother me... but it's not like you've ever hung out with us before. And what about Foster? Are you two fighting or something? Because it feels like you are."

My fingers drift to the collar of my shirt where the locket is tucked away. "No. Foster and I... We aren't anything."

His gaze tracks the movement and question marks flood his eyes. "What does that mean? Because for as long as I can remember, you guys have been best friends."

I decide what to do next. I could just keep tiptoeing around the truth. I've always been pretty good at that, at pretending—I can see that now. But honestly, I'm getting tired of it. Tired of the lies, of being lied to, of being a liar myself. So, taking a deep breath, I pull out the necklace and let it rest on the outside of my shirt.

"I found this in Foster's room the other night," I tell him. "It's a necklace I lost when I was six. It was that day Foster wanted to dig a hole in the backyard of my house, and you took the fall when we got caught. I'm not sure if you remember, but I lost the necklace in the forest when Foster and I were looking for something to bury in the hole. When I realized it was gone, Foster supposedly went back into the forest to look for it. But he said he couldn't find it. He looked for it for weeks after that, but supposedly he could never find it. But then there it was in his room, tucked away in a book."

Kingsley smashes his lips together, his gaze burrowing into mine. He doesn't say anything, but it looks like he wants to.

"What?" I press, resting my arms on the back of the seat.

Strands of his hair fall into his eyes as he shakes his head. "I didn't say anything."

"But you want to."

"Yeah, but wanting something and actually getting it doesn't exist in my world." He smashes his lips together. "You know what? Forget I said that." He shoves the door open and bails out of the car.

I practically dive out and rush after him.

Porter shouts something about us having a lover's quarrel, but I ignore him, hurrying to catch up with Kingsley as he reaches the entrance doors of the gas station.

"What did you mean by that?" I ask.

He keeps on ignoring me, yanking open the door. But I capture his wrist, stopping him, and my fingertips end up pressed against his pulse.

We both freeze.

"Your heart's beating so fast," I whisper.

He tenses, shifting his arm, and I expect him to pull away. But instead, he slides his fingers down my arm to my bandaged wrist. Then he turns, his gaze welding with mine, and my heart pounds inside my chest. *Throbs.*

A haziness starts to spin through my mind, my gaze falling to his lips.

His warm lips on mine...

Breathing air into my lungs...

I want to kiss him...

Breathe him in and taste him.

I start to stand on my tiptoes to do just that.

Kingsley's lips part.

"I want..." He breathes out, his chest rising and crashing.

I'm about to say I want it to, but then he jerks away from me and mutters, "I need to piss."

Then he dashes inside the building, leaving me standing there, stunned.

Not only because he basically just ran away from me, but because I just about kissed him.

I'm not sure what just came over me. I barely know Kingsley, and up until a few days ago, I thought he was gorgeous but dangerous. And when I tried to kiss him, my mind felt hazy yet at the same time, clear. It doesn't make any sense.

And what about Foster? I know I'm angry with him, but I need to confront him. I've always been a bit afraid of confrontation, though, especially with Foster. I can see that now, my avoidance to demand the truth from him, my... fear of him?

No, I'm not afraid of Foster.

Am I?

TWENTY
HARLYNN

When I enter the gas station, Kingsley is nowhere to be seen. I assume he's in the bathroom taking a "piss" like he said. Although, he could've made that up so he could bail out on me trying to kiss him.

Reality crashes over me as I realize how awkward I may have made things between Kingsley and me.

"Great, this night is about to get even more awkward than it already is," I mutter as I pass by the register.

The cashier is the same guy that was working the night of the accident, and he gives me a funny look, like he thinks I'm insane. At this point, I'm thinking the same thing.

I give him a small smile then head down the candy aisle. Memories of that night float around me, of Porter teasing me, of me touching Kingsley's arm, and how

Foster was so irritated about it, how he said Kingsley had been flirting with me.

Then my thoughts shift to later on, when I found Foster in here after he lost his wallet. How Beth had been in the aisle crying.

"I was a mess that night, wasn't I?"

Beth's voice rolls over my shoulder.

What in the hell?

I start to turn toward her. "Hey, did you know everyone thinks you're..." The words fade on my tongue as my gaze lands on her.

I blink a few times, certain I'm hallucinating. But what I'm seeing remains.

Beth is standing in front of me, her clothes are torn, her skin is smudged with dirt and blood, and her lips are dark blue. Her hair is covered with twigs and blood trickles from her forehead.

"What happened to you?" I whisper in horror.

Her lips twist into a numb smile. "You don't know the answer to that already?"

"Why would I?"

She doesn't respond. She doesn't even blink.

"Everyone's looking for you," I tell her. "Are you okay?"

"Do I look okay?" she questions, elevating her brows.

"No. You look like your hurt." I eye the blood trickling

from her head. "I think you might need to go to the hospital."

"Why? They can't help me. No one can except for you." She stares at me in a way that makes the hairs on my arms stand on end.

"Why me?" I ask nervously.

Her twisted smile looks all sorts of wrong. "Because you died and came back. But you came back wrong—or right depending on how you want to look at it—and now you can see the truth."

Is she crazy? "I... I don't know what you're talking about? What truth?"

She grins, revealing a mouth full of chipped teeth. "Can't you see it? It's right in front of you?"

My gaze sweeps the mostly empty gas station. "There's nothing here—"

A drop of water splatters against my forehead. My gaze drifts to the ceiling. A huge water stain stains the tile and the light is flickering on and off.

I swipe the water from my head and return my attention to Beth. Her mouth is agape and her tongue is missing. I trip backward, and end up smacking my elbow against the shelf behind me.

"You can't run from the truth." Her lips remain frozen as she speaks. "It lives inside you." Then she lets out a blood-curdling scream, water spewing from her mouth.

I whirl around to run, but my feet are glued to the floor. Water gushes around me, filling up the gas station and rising to my knees. I open my mouth to scream, but my lips are cinched shut.

I am helpless.

I can't move.

I am going to die here.

I am alone.

No one is here with me.

Alone...

I'm in this truck alone.

Foster is gone and only darkness surrounds me.

I press my head against the inside of the roof of the truck as the water consumes the cab.

I can't see anything but darkness and water.

I can't swim.

And soon the water is going to take over the truck.

This truck is going to be my tomb.

I close my eyes and brace myself for the end—

Fingers thread through mine and a hand brushes my cheek.

"I've got you," someone whispers. "I promise I won't let anything happen to you."

I start to open my eyes, desperate to see their face. When I see their eyes, I gasp—

I jerk back, gasping for air, only to realize I'm standing

in the gas station, not sinking in the lake again. There is no water around me. My savior is gone. Beth isn't here anymore either, only the cashier guy who's staring at me like I just sprouted a unicorn horn out of my ass.

He warily eyes me over from the other side of the counter. "Are you okay?"

I attempt to nod, but my head won't cooperate. "I don't know."

"Are you on something?" he questions with an arch of his brow. "If you are, you need to leave the store. I don't need any more damn kids coming in here high and then my ass gets in trouble when they disappear. Like I can control that shit."

"What're talking about?" I hug my arms around myself as I shuffle up the aisle toward him, confused.

So confused.

Always confused.

His eyes narrow at me. "Like you already don't know."

"I... I really don't."

He considers what I said with a scowl. "That girl your boyfriend was talking to in here the other night—Beth, I think her name is—went missing. And since this was the last place she was seen and according to some witnesses, she was high while she was here, the police think I had something to do with her disappearance. Funny thing is, the only people that saw her when she was here was your boyfriend, the guys you just pulled in here with, and you, so my bet is one of you told the police to come question me."

What? "I didn't—"

"I don't want to hear your bullshit lies," he cuts me off, lifting his hand. "Just get what you need and take your high ass out of my store."

"I'm not high," I mumble, although I kind of wish I was. At least then I'd have an excuse for what I just saw.

I suck in a gradual breath as the image of Beth, dirty, bloody, and broken sears my mind.

What was that? A hallucination?

But it felt so real.

Inhaling and exhaling, I turn to leave.

"And FYI, your little boyfriend, the one with the smartass mouth, is a liar," the cashier calls out after me.

I stop dead in my tracks and twist back around. "Why would you say that?"

"Because he never lost his wallet that night. He came in here, threw it down on the counter, and told me to give it to him when he asked for it. The asshole didn't even wait for me to agree to do it. Then he went into the bathroom with that Beth chick. My guess is to fuck her. Well, either that or get high with her. Either way, your boyfriend's a liar. And probably a cheater." He seems so pleased with himself that he's telling me all these horrible things.

It should piss me off that he's being so awful. But what he's saying... What happened that night...

Memories stain the air around me like shadows of a past I can barely recall.

Beth had been crying when I'd come back into the gas station the second time. And she had been flirting and talking to Foster earlier. Could he have said something to upset her?

A chill spills across my flesh as another thought occurs to me.

Could Foster have something to do with Beth's disappearance?

I shake my head. No. Foster was with me on the cliff that night. Still, that doesn't mean the cashier is lying. That Foster didn't do something with Beth the second time he entered the gas station. What was he doing, though? Getting high with her? I'd accused him of being stoned a handful of times that night, but I never really believed it. And he never really seemed stoned.

What other reason does that leave? That he was screwing Beth in the bathroom like the cashier implied. That'd mean he had sex with her right before he kissed me and told me he loved me.

A couple of weeks ago, I'd have been positive that couldn't be true, but now...

Tears well in my eyes. I haven't cried in weeks and the sensation feels foreign and strange. I feel so off balance, like I'm about to fall over. And I'll keep falling and falling and falling down into an abyss.

Sucking back the tears, I run out of the gas station. Not wanting Porter to see me crying, I veer around to the side of the building. But the moment I round the corner, I regret my decision and slam to a halt.

Just a handful of feet away from me, Kingsley is standing by a dumpster, and beside him is Porter along with a guy who has the hood of his jacket drawn over his head.

I'm so confused. I never saw Kingsley leave the gas station, but maybe he slipped out the back door. Why, though?

"Look, I'm not sure how long I can do this," Kingsley says as he roughly tugs his fingers through his hair. "It's starting to take over my entire life."

"I know it's frustrating," the stranger replies, reclining back against the wall of the gas station and lighting up a cigarette. "But you agreed to do this. Now you can always back out of the deal, but you'll have to pay the consequences."

Kingsley shakes his head. "I fucking hate this... Lying

to everyone... to her." He sighs. "But I get it. I did this to myself."

"Yeah, you did," the guy agrees, a cloud of smoke puffing from his lips.

"Oh, shut the fuck up, Evan," Porter snaps, stuffing his hands into his back pockets. "Just because you have that stupid badge, doesn't mean you're better than us."

Badge? Like a cop badge?

The stranger—Evan pushes from the wall. "Maybe I should go over the list of reasons why you're here and see if you still think that."

Porter inches toward him with his fists curled at his sides. I sense a fight about to break out and I start to back away, but bump into a solid, cold object.

"Don't run from him. Trust him," Beth whispers in my ear.

Then I'm shoved forward.

I stumble, bumping my arm into the side of the building, but quickly regain my balance and push away from the wall. I throw a panicked glance behind me, hoping to all the stars that Beth is behind me. A human, very alive Beth. But nope. Nothing but darkness is there.

"Har, what're you doing?" Kingsley asks with an edge in his tone.

He's nervous.

That thought comes out of nowhere, but somehow I know...

Kingsley is nervous.

I slowly turn back around. "Um... I... I thought you had to piss?"

Jesus, out of everything I could say, those are the words I go with.

Nice, Harlynn. Really smooth.

Porter gives me a funny look then flicks a glance at Kingsley. "Dude, you told her you had to piss?"

Kingsley presses him with a look and Porter frowns, his gaze sliding to Evan, who's observing me closely. I can tell that he's a bit older than me with a scruffy jawline and an intense gaze. The kind of gaze my dad sometimes gets when he's trying to figure out what to do with me after I've done something wrong.

Great. What in the hell did I just interrupt? A drug exchange or something?

But Porter said Evan has a badge. I guess cops can deal drugs, though. Although that wouldn't make this situation any better.

"I'm going to go wait in the car," I mutter, then spin around to haul ass away from them.

Fingers fold around my arm before I can make it very far. I tense as Kingsley steers me back around to face him.

His gaze skims across my face then a frown forms on his lips. "Were you crying just barely?"

I wipe my eyes with the sleeve of my jacket. "No, I have allergies," I lie.

He shakes his head, but doesn't say anything else about it. "Go wait in the car, okay? Porter and I just need to finish this up and then we can go." His tone is surprisingly soft.

I nod, then high tail it away from there, walking straight to Porter's car. Then I climb into the backseat and start conjuring up a plan of what I'm going to do. Should I pretend like I didn't see anything? Or should I ask Kingsley and Porter what that was about? It was pretty clear I wasn't supposed to overhear that conversation, and the old Harlynn would just let this go. But this new Harlynn wants the truth. How am I supposed to see the truth, though, when everyone around me keeps painting the air with lies? And all I can seem to do is breathe them in. Breathe in their lies, over and over again, letting them pollute my lungs and my mind.

Maybe that's why I'm hallucinating Beth. Because my mind is so damn polluted with lies.

"Am I a hallucination, though?" She materializes in the seat beside me.

I squeeze my eyes shut. "You're not real."

"Maybe not to everyone," she says. "But to you I may very well be the realest thing in your life right now."

"What does that mean?"

"It means you can't trust anyone. Not until you can see the truth."

"What is the truth, though?" I whisper.

"There's a lot of truth's, Harlynn, but right here might be a good start." She brushes her icy-cold fingers across my arm, drawing them downward and along the bandage on my wrist.

Then she pulls back and silence settles over me.

I crack my eyes open to find her gone.

My gaze drops to the bandage that conceals the feather-like wound. How can this be the start of the truth? What is this wound?

An idea comes to me and I dig my phone out of my pocket. Then I do a search on mysterious feather-shaped wounds. A few articles pop up and I start skim reading them. About the third article in, I stumble onto something that piques my interest:

A feather-shaped wound, also known as the Sight of Fallen Darkness, usually appears after someone has briefly slipped past the veil that divides the Land of the Living and the World of the Alive. The person who bears the mark has seen what lies in death. A handful of people with the mark have reported having certain abilities, most of which are related to, but aren't limited to, being able to communicate with the dead, which some refer to as necromancy. Many psychics have the mark, but that doesn't mean all who bare the mark can see the future.

After that, the article shifts focus to psychic abilities, something I'm fairly certain I don't have. But necromancy... communicating with the dead...

A shudder rolls through my body.

Is Beth not a hallucination? Am I really talking to her?

Talking to her from the grave?

And does that mean Beth is dead?

TWENTY-ONE
HARLYNN

I remain in the car by myself for a bit, waiting for Beth to appear again, but she never does. Eventually my thoughts drift to the dream I had last night about Paige. Paige who was just found dead in the lake. Does that mean that somehow I'm communicating with her too?

Goosebumps sprout across my flesh and I shiver. If I can communicate with the dead, just how bad is this going to get? How many spirits are going to appear to me? And what about the incident in the gas station where I thought the entire place filled up with water and I was slammed back into a memory of that night in the lake? Is stuff like that going to happen to me more frequently?

My temples pound as my mind races with so many thoughts I can barely keep up with them. The wound on my wrist pulsates with pain to the point where I feel sick.

I may have very well thrown up all over the floor of Porter's car, but when him and Kingsley open the doors and climb in, strangely, the pain dissolves.

The second the doors shut, Kingsley rotates around in his seat, his lips parting. But then his eyes skim across my face and worry creases his features. "Are you okay?"

I nod, lowering my fingers from my temples. "I just have—or well, had a headache."

But it went away when you climbed in.

The worry remains on his face. "Do you want to go get some painkillers from the gas station—"

"No," I say way too quickly. When Kingsley's brows rise at my outburst, I add, "Sorry, I'm just... The cashier in there was being a jerk and I don't want to deal with him again."

Kingsley glances at the gas station. So does Porter.

"Looks like Will's working tonight," Porter mutters, his gaze shifting to Kingsley.

They trade an indecipherable look then both their gazes slide to me.

"You want us to teach him a lesson, dead girl?" Porter asks with a hint of amusement.

"No," I start to say but then pause. "Wait... What do you mean by that?"

Porter's amusement doubles and Kingsley lets out a weighted sigh.

"Porter," Kingsley warns, but Porter talks over him.

"What do you think it means?" Porter rests his elbow on the back of the seat as he turns to look at me. "Come on, dead girl, let us hear just how bad you think we are."

Normally, I'd throw a snarky comeback at him. But with everything that's happened over the last fifteen minutes, my minds too exhausted to banter right now.

"Who was that guy you were talking to over there?" I change the subject, pointing in the direction of the side of the gas station.

The smile fizzles from Porter's lips and Kingsley's frown deepens.

"It's just some guy we know," Kingsley replies evasively while Porter looks away and starts up the engine.

My gaze bounces back and forth between the two of them. I note how shifty they are. My initial instinct is to back off, but Beth's voice purrs in my ear.

"Ask them," she whispers. "You can't get to the truth if you don't ask for it."

"I've been trying to ask for it," I mutter underneath my breath. "No one will tell me anything."

Kingsley glances over his shoulder at me with his brows knit. "What?"

"Nothing." Jesus, I'm one step away from looking like I need to be locked up in a padded room. "Seriously, though, what were you guys doing with that Evan guy?"

Kingsley looks away from me, fiddling with a leather band on his wrist. "We were just talking to him. And his name's not really Evan. That's just what we call him."

I chew on my bottom lip, trying to convince myself to shut the hell up, but apparently my mouth has taken on a mind of it's own. "What did he mean by if you backed out, you'd have to pay the consequences? Are you... dealing drugs or something?"

Porter's grip on the wheel tightens and a muscle in Kingsley's jaw ticks. Nervousness edges through me, but when Kingsley gaze locks with mine, my anxiety lulls back to sleep.

"Look, as much as I wish I could tell you what that was about, I can't," he says, appearing apologetic. "But I promise it's not as bad as you're probably thinking. And while this is going to make the situation sound even sketchier, I really need you to just let this go for now and not bring it up to anyone. Not the conversation you heard. Not the guy you saw us with." His eyes silently plead with me. "Please, Har."

How can I say no when he's looking at me like that?

"You promise it's not bad?" I ask and he nods. I hitch out my pinkie in front of me. "Pinkie swear it then."

A soft smile graces his lips. While I haven't done the

pinkie swearing thing with Kingsley as much as I have with Foster, we did it a couple of times when we were younger and still hung out sometimes. We even did it when he gave me my very first kiss, and he pinkie swore that my fish was in a better place...

"I promise it's not suffering," he assures me after I confessed to him that I'm worried death is hurting the fish.

I sniffle. "You swear it?"

He sticks out his pinkie in front of him. "I pinkie swear it."

I smile, feeling a bit better already. Pinkie swearing means he's telling the truth. So, I hitch my pinkie with his.

After we release each other's pinkies, I start crying again, though.

"What's wrong?" he asks worriedly.

Tears drip down my cheeks as I stare at the shoebox in front of us where my dead fish is. "I just miss her and I feel bad that she died... It was my fault."

He glances from the box to my face then reaches over and slips his fingers through mine. Like every time he touches me, he trembles a bit.

"I'm sorry you're hurting." He brushes away some tears from my cheeks with the back of his hand. Then with an uneven breath, he leans forward and places a soft kiss against my cheek. "And it's not your fault," he whispers.

"You're the sweetest person I know, Har. You've never done anything to intentionally hurt anything or anyone."

My heart is like a butterfly in my chest, but I feel so much better...

I frown as the weight of what Kingsley said in that moment crushes my chest.

Back then, he thought I was the kind of person who'd never intentionally hurt anything or anyone. Only a couple of years later, the incident on the dock happened and I pretty much stopped talking to him. It makes me wonder what he thinks of me now.

But maybe I can change that. Be a better person.

I hitch my pinkie with his and his fingers trembles ever so slightly, like the last time we made a pinkie promise. But unlike the last time, his gaze is so intense I swear I can feel it searing into my soul.

"Thank you." My voice is surprisingly steady. "And thank you for letting me hang out with you tonight."

"You don't have to thank me for that," he says. "And I'm sorry if I acted like a jerk earlier. I just..."

"Have serious social issues," Porter chimes in, meeting my gaze in the rearview mirror. "I blame it on his brother. Foster fucked his head up big time. And his parents aren't any better. But I think you already know that."

"Shut up, man," Kingsley shoots him an icy glare.

"Unless you want me to air out your family's drama in front of her."

That wipes the smile right off Porter's face. "All right, I'll stop."

Kingsley relaxes a smidgeon until his gaze fastens onto our interlocked pinkies. Then he swallows hard but doesn't pull away, scratching at the side of his neck.

"You can let go if you want to," I tell him, even though I don't want him to.

What I want is to feel calm and touching him is making me feel that way.

If I could, I might touch him forever.

Rubbing his lips together, he gradually pulls his pinkie away from mine. The moment our skin breaks contact, a numbness seeps through my body.

Cold.

Dead.

Empty, except for the sporadic sensation of confusion.

Why do I feel this way most of the time?

Better yet, why do I only not feel this way whenever I'm around Kingsley?

TWENTY-TWO
HARLYNN

The party ends up being not too far away from the gas station, near a log cabin in the forest and about a few miles away from the lake. While I can't actually see the large body of water that almost devoured me that night, I can smell the scent of moss and moisture in the air, a reminder that it's not too far away, haunting me with memories, not just of myself, but of Paige.

Images of that dream I had of her briefly flash through my mind as Porter parks at the end of a long row of cars and rolls down the window, letting the scent of lake water creep into the cab. Once he's parked, he climbs out. Kingsley follows suit, getting out too, and flips the seat up to let me out.

As I lower my head to duck out, I end up tripping over

my untied bootlaces and almost eat a mouthful of dirt. But Kingsley catches me and stops me from falling.

His fingers slide down my arm to steady me and my pulse quickens. *Safe, safe, safe*, I swear it whispers to me. Then he withdraws his hand and my heart rate settles, murmuring *cold, cold, cold*.

I glance up at Kingsley, wondering if he can feel any of this, but he's not even looking at me, his gaze fixed on the fire and the people surrounding it.

Almost everyone here is holding either a beer bottle or a cup. Some people are smoking, some are making out, and some are dancing to the music blasting from a stereo.

"You should probably remind dead girl of the rules," Porter tells Kingsley as he rounds the front of the car, stuffing his keys into his pocket.

"What rules?" I ask but then pause. "Wait, is this like the last party I went to with you guys? The one that had the no drinking or smoking anything rule?"

It's the first time I've actually spoken directly about that party with them, and surprisingly, I don't feel as ashamed as I thought I would. Then again, the girl who thought she'd feel ashamed might not even exist anymore.

Kingsley turns to me, his face a shadow against the night. "Yes, please, don't drink or smoke anything anyone gives you, okay?" He scratches at his wrist, his gaze bouncing from the fire then back to me. "In fact, you should try to avoid drinking anything at all while we're here?"

"What if I get thirsty?"

"Then tell me and I'll get you a drink."

"But then wouldn't that technically be breaking the rules, since I'd be drinking the drink you gave me?"

Porter smirks at me. "Such a smartass."

I flip him off but he only laughs then strolls off toward a group of people.

I redirect my attention back to Kingsley and find him frowning at me.

"Har, I promise you can trust me," he swears, the fire reflecting against the intensity in his eyes. "I wouldn't ever do anything that would hurt you."

"I know." The words—they feel so true.

Truer than anything else in my life at the moment.

It's crazy, though, trusting him this much when I know he's harboring a secret from me. But I can't seem to make the sensation fade away.

A smile starts to touch his lips, but he hastily erases the look and turns around, hiking toward the fire. His bootlaces are untied like mine and I find myself smiling over the similarity. But my smile quickly evaporates as I become aware that I'm standing in front of Porter's car by myself, and almost all of the faces around me are unfamiliar. I've never been one to just walk up and try to make small talk with someone I don't know. That's always been Foster's thing. I could follow Kingsley, but he didn't invite me to. And there's no way in hell I'm going to tag along with Porter.

I deliberate climbing back into the car and hiding out in there, but that won't help me get any closer to the truth. And besides, the old Harlynn would've climbed in the car and hid, and I don't want to be her anymore.

I slide my foot forward and slowly head toward the crowd, telling myself I can handle this. Halfway there, Kingsley slows to a stop, turns back around, and scans the area. When his eyes land on me, a crease forms between his brows.

"You coming?" he asks.

While I may have just grown the ladyballs to endeavor into the party on my own, I'm grateful for his offer and hurry over to him.

"What were you doing?" he asks when I reach him.

"I wasn't sure if you wanted to hang out with me or do your own thing, so..." I lift a shoulder.

He sweeps strands of his hair out of his eyes. "Why would we invite you here if we didn't want to hang out with you?"

"Well technically you didn't invite me," I remind him. "In fact, you said that if you knew Porter was picking me up beforehand, you wouldn't have let him."

"Yeah, you're right." He fiddles with the chain dangling from his belt loop. "I'm sorry I said that. It just kind of took me by surprise when he showed up at your house. Plus... I worry about you hanging out with us."

My brows pull together. "Why?"

He works his jaw from side to side as he stares at the fire. "I just don't want you getting involved in the shit that is my life right now."

I sink my teeth into my bottom lip as I assess his profile, the sorrow haunting his eyes, the fullness of his lips.

God, he's so beautiful.

I've thought this about him before, but felt guilty about it, like there was something wrong with my mind. In this moment, though, without Foster around, the guilt isn't present.

"Why is your life shit right now?" I ask. 'Is it... Does it have to do with that Evan guy?"

He scuffs the tip of his boot against the dirt. "It has to do with a lot of things."

"And you can't tell me what these things are? Not even a little bit?"

He shakes his head and sighs. "No, I really can't." He stops kicking the dirt and straightens his stance, his gaze finding mine. "Come on. Let's go do this party thing."

His swift shift in topic gives me a bit of whiplash, but

I hurry after him as he walks into the crowd. People are standing so close to one another that we have to push our way through. I've never been one for being in crowds and claustrophobia starts to set in. As if he's in sync with my emotions, Kingsley reaches back and takes ahold of my hand. His fingers tremble as he tugs me forward, guiding me around until I'm right in front of him. Then he places his hands on my hips and steers me forward, using his elbows to create a path.

My claustrophobia dissipates and is replaced by the butterfly sensation I got when he kissed me on the cheek all those years ago. His chest is pressed against my back and I swear I can feel his heart beating as rapidly as mine. The scent of him engulfs me, along with his warmth.

Safe. Safe. Safe.

I very well may have been content staying that way forever, just me and him in the middle of the throng of people, with his hands on my hips, my heart beating deafeningly in my chest, the feeling of being *alive* dancing in the air. But eventually, we arrive at the edge of the crowd and he withdraws his hands from my hips.

A quiet sigh leaves my lips, but the music swallows the sound up.

"Sorry about that." Kingsley moves up beside me. "I remembered about halfway in that you get claustrophobic around a lot of people. Well, unless that's changed."

"No, it hasn't. I'm surprised you remembered, though."

He shrugs then turns toward a table with a bunch of bottles and cans on it. "You had that panic attack that one time when we were at a carnival and it was super crowded. When I asked why you were panicking, you told me you get scared when you're around a lot of people. I made a mental note of it so I could make sure it never happened again." He eyes over the drink selection. "I think I was too young to realize that we wouldn't always be around each other so I couldn't always protect you."

Protect.

Porter had said the other day that I had my very own protector, implying that Kingsley was it. Maybe he was right.

When Kingsley looks at me, his brows furrow. "What's wrong?"

"It's nothing. This is just... nice."

His confusion grows. "What is?"

I shrug. "Hanging out with you." When uncertainty floods his eyes, I ask, "What?"

Shaking his head, he picks up a bottle and fiddles with the lid. "It's nothing."

"No, it's something." When he makes no effort to respond or even look at me, I steal the bottle from his hand.

His gaze darts to me then he grabs the bottle from me, frantically peering around. Then he leans in to whisper in my ear, "Remember, no drinking anything unless it's from me."

I resist a shiver as his breath dusts across my skin. "I wasn't going to. I was just trying to get you to tell me why you're annoyed that I said it was nice hanging out with you."

"Oh." He slants back, scratching his head. "It doesn't annoy me."

"Liar. I can tell it does."

"I swear it doesn't." He sets the bottle back onto the table. "I just wonder if Foster was here, if you'd even be standing here talking to me." He can barely look at me as he says it.

The barely is enough to make me feel a tremendous amount of guilt.

"I'm sorry for cutting you out of my life. There was just a lot of stuff that happened over the years that made me question whether or not I should be friends with you." I sink my teeth into my bottom lip. Saying the words aloud makes me feel awful. "I was stupid, though, for being confused about it. I should've been friends with you. I can see that now."

He stares at me, his expression unreadable. "What stuff happened to make you feel that way?"

I consider telling him about what Foster told me all those years ago, but that might start a fight between him and Kingsley, and I don't want to be the cause of that. But being a liar doesn't feel like a great choice either.

"It has to do with Foster, doesn't it?" he says before I can come up with an answer.

The lack of emotion in his voice makes me question how long he's thought this.

"No," I start, but then the lie burns on my tongue. "Yes... Maybe... I don't know." I blow out a stressed breath. "I don't want to start a fight between you two."

"You won't," he assures me. When I lift a brow, he adds, "I wasn't lying about what I said in the gas station the other day. I don't start fights with Foster. He just hates me. Always has."

"That's not true. He doesn't hate you. You guys just don't get along—"

"No, he hates me," he cuts me off, his tone resolute. "He has since the day he realized I wasn't going to do whatever he wanted. It was around the time we started being friends with you and he told me you were going to be his friend, not mine. When I wouldn't agree to that, he got irritated and told my mom that the hole I dug in your backyard—you remember that hole?" He doesn't wait for me to finish, anger flashing in his eyes. "He told her that I said I was going to bury you in that hole. I wasn't allowed to see you for an entire month because of that and by then, you and Foster were already friends. And I had to go to therapy because my parents thought I was crazy." He smashes his lips together, his fingers trembling as his hands ball into fists. "I'm sorry. I don't need to put my shit on you."

It feels like the ground is about to open up and swallow me whole. Like my life is one big lie. The sad part is, only weeks ago, I wouldn't have believed Kingsley. But now, after Foster lied about saving me, after I found the necklace, after what the cashier said to me, I can see the truth. That my best friend—ex-best friend is a fucking liar. And with Foster being so tied to every aspect of my past, it makes me feel like I've been living a nightmare for the last eighteen years and I'm just waking up. Perhaps death did that to me. Perhaps I was sleepwalking through all those years, and when death seized me by the lungs, it woke me up—screamed at me to see. Perhaps who ever breathed life into me, breathed me into another life.

Before I can tell Kingsley any of this, though—well not all of it, but some—he stalks away toward the trees, muttering, "I'm such a fucking idiot."

Snapping out of my shock, I chase after him, grabbing his arm right before he reaches the trees. He grinds to a halt, tension rippling from his body. I try not to take it offensively and skitter around to stand in front of him.

"You're not an idiot," I insist. He won't meet my gaze, staring over my shoulder, his dark eyes so damn haunted it nearly tears my soul in half. Mustering up every damn ounce of courage I have, I mold my palm to his cheek and force him to look at me. "You're not an idiot," I repeat and his throat muscles bob as he swallows hard. "I am." He starts to shake his head, but I refuse to let him, my hand remaining firm on his cheek. "I'm an idiot for believing Foster. For not making my own choices. For not being able to see what was really going on. But I can see it now. I really can."

His hesitant gaze searches mine. "I don't want to sound like an asshole, but I don't get it." He steps back, roughly tugging his fingers through his hair, and making the strands go askew. My hand falls lifelessly to my side, already aching to touch his skin again. "I mean, it's always been Foster. Always... It's why I never said..." He sucks in a gradual breath. "And now you're here, telling me you believe me, not him. It just... It doesn't make sense."

"It kind of does, though, if you really think about it," I mutter, eliciting a questioning look from him. I sigh, knowing I can either tell him the truth or continue tiptoeing around it. And I'm tired of tiptoeing—tired of lying.

Liar.

Liar.

Liar.

I've been a liar for so long. I'm realizing that now. That even before the accident, I lied about how I felt, what I thought. Who I really was.

"I already told you about the necklace I found in Foster's room," I say. "And about how he's been lying about having it for all these years. Well, I also found out there's other stuff he's been lying to me about too."

"Like what?" he wonders. When I don't answer right away, he adds, "Not that I'm questioning you. I know my brother lies all the time."

"No, you're fine." I hug my arms around myself as the wind picks up. "It's just one of the things is going to make me sound a bit weird."

"Har, I may not be a lot of things, but weird definitely isn't one of them. Trust me, whatever you say, I'll be cool with it."

"Even if I tried to convince you there was a unicorn right behind you?" I crack a nervous joke.

The corners of his lips twitch upward. "Wouldn't be the first time. And can I point out that the last time you said something like that to me, you almost convinced me it was true."

My lips pull into a smile. "Holy crap, I almost forgot about that."

We were seven and hanging out alone while Foster was at a soccer game.

My mom had been babysitting Kingsley and we'd been telling scary stories about ghosts living in the forest. When I got too scared, I tried to convince Kingsley that there were really unicorns living in there.

His reply: "You might be right. The other day I thought I saw a sparkly horse running around in the trees."

I thought he was being serious. Looking back, I think he was trying to comfort me because he knew the ghost stories were scaring me.

"I think you were just trying to make me feel better for being scared and almost crying," I tell him.

He shakes his head. "No way. I totally thought I saw a sparkling horse."

"Liar."

"Nonbeliever."

A laugh bursts from my lips, but then a sigh replaces it. If only he knew how wrong he is, that I believe in a lot of things, that I'm starting to believe in ghosts. And that I can talk to them.

I wonder if he'd think I was crazy if I told him all of this.

"I'm pretty sure Foster is lying about saving me that night," I find myself whispering.

The wind picks up, blowing strands of my hair into my face, but I make no move to pluck them out. When he continues to stand there motionless, a shadow beneath the moonlight, I open my mouth to ask him what he's thinking, if he thinks I'm wrong.

But words leave his lips first.

"I think..." he trails off, his posture stiffening as a guy with shoulder-length blonde hair approaches us.

"Kings, my man, you flying tonight?" he greets Kingsley with a chin nod.

The tightness in Kingsley's muscles amplifies, his gaze flitting to me then back to the stranger. "Yeah, but not here." He gives a nod in the direction of Porter's car. "Go over there. I'll be there in a sec."

The guy notes me with a glance, his gaze lazily scrolling up and down my body. "You coming too?"

"No." Kingsley's tone is like ice and the guy immediately steps back with his hands raised in front of him.

"Sorry, my bad." He doesn't make eye contact with me as he turns around and hikes toward Porter's car.

Kingsley releases an audible sigh then glances at me, his expression guarded.

"I need to go take care of something," he tells me as he shucks off his jacket. "I'll be right back. If you need me, text me. And please don't drink or smoke anything, okay?" He hands me his jacket.

I take it. "What's this for?"

"Because you're cold," he replies simply.

"Oh." Again, I question how in tune he is with me. "Thanks."

He offers me a small smile, but a frown pulls at his lips as he walks away, the moment we shared dissipating. But then he pauses and glances over his shoulder at me.

"When I get back, I think I need to tell you something," he says. "About the night of the accident. I just hope you can forgive me."

My heart thumps deafeningly in my chest as I nod. Then he walks away, leaving me with my thoughts and my soaring pulse.

What does he need to tell me? Does he know what happened the night of the accident? But how? He wasn't there that night. I saw him driving in the opposite direction when he left the gas station.

I sigh and slip on Kingsley's jacket, aware that once again I'm sinking into the Land of Confusion. Warmth seeps through my body along with the scent of his cologne mixed with a hint of smoke. I breathe the scent in, pulling the jacket tighter as the wind picks up, leaves and dirt blowing through the air.

"Standing around isn't going to get you to the truth."

I tense as Beth's voice gusts over my shoulder. A slamming heartbeat of a second later, she steps up beside me, her sunken in eyes locked on the mob of people in front of us.

"Look at all of them," she remarks. "They think they're so happy."

"They look happy," I whisper. "Most of them are either smiling or laughing."

"But is it real?" She tilts her head toward me, her bones making a god awful creaking noise.

"It looks real."

"On the outside, maybe. But all of this—it's just a mask. An illusion created so you'll let your guard down. I can see that now."

"See what exactly?"

"The truth."

"You keep talking about the truth like you know what it is, but if you do, why can't you tell me?" I ask in frustration.

Her hollow eyes lock on me. "Because I've been silenced."

Suddenly, I can feel it, a roaring wave—her pain, the agony inside her.

"What happened to you?" I whisper. "Are you... Are you a ghost?"

She doesn't respond, stepping toward the crowd. A voice inside my mind begs me to follow her, a voice that I'm not positive belongs to me. But I obey, trailing after her, fighting my anxiety as I enter the madness. I become very aware that not a single person glances in her direction, as if she's not there. A couple of people do notice me as I squeeze by, including Liam, one of Foster's friends.

"Harlynn?" His gaze sweeps the area then lands on me, his brows creasing. "Where's Foster?"

"He's not here." My gaze shifts between him and Beth as she continues to slip further into the crowd.

Shit, if I'm going to follow her, I'm going to have to fight my anxiety on my own.

He scratches his forehead. "So you just came here by yourself?"

His surprise is annoying, but I don't have time to get irritated. Not when Beth is moving further away from me.

I throw him a wave and walk away. I have a feeling, though, that soon, I'm going to receive a text from Foster, asking me why I'm at a party without him. And at a party that's filled with people associated with Kingsley. Maybe he'll even figure out I'm with Kingsley and Porter.

Sure enough, only a handful of seconds later, my phone vibrates from inside my pocket. I ignore it, quickening my pace and stumbling through the mob of sweaty, drunken people, my pulse soaring. I'm on the verge of hyperventilating and I nearly turn back several times, but my desire for the truth keeps me moving forward.

Finally, after what feels like hours, but is probably

only about a minute, I stumble from the crowd and out onto the stretch of land just in front of the forest.

Beth is there, waiting for me at the edge of the trees. She glances at me, the moonlight highlighting the eerie smile on her face. Then she steps into the forest and blends in with the night.

I hesitate. I've never been a huge fan of the dark. Plus, I'd be wandering in there alone, which seems stupid considering all the disappearances plaguing the town. I may have very well turned around, but a familiar voice touches my ears.

"Will you just shut up and do it," Star says, her voice floating over from the trees. "I'm getting bored."

"I'm trying," a guy replies in a haste. "But it's freakin' dark in here."

Star.

Star is here.

Star, the girl who may know a truth I seek.

I inch toward the trees. "Star?"

The air grows still except for the laughter and music drifting over from the party.

"Crazy girl?" She stumbles from the shadows of the forest.

Or well, I think it's Star. She looks a lot thinner than I remember, her hair is black now, and she's wearing worn, oversized clothes.

"Hey." I try to mask the shock over her altered appearance.

A smile breaks out across her face as she walks toward me. "What're you doing here? Not that I'm upset about it. But this isn't your normal scene."

"I came with Porter and Kingsley," I tell her, tucking my hands into the sleeves of Kingsley's jacket as the air grows chillier.

A look of what can only be described as amused shock passes across her face. "So you're hanging out with Kingsley now, huh?"

I waver. "Yeah, I guess so."

She grins. "It's about damn time. I thought that boy was never going to get over his whole I'm-not-good-enough-for-Harlynn issue. Not that I'm surprised he thinks that way with how his family treats him." A frown flashes across her face but she hastily puts on a smile. "But anyway, tell me everything. How did he ask you out? Are you guys officially dating? I heard you got into an accident. Are you okay?" Her lips are moving so quickly that I can barely keep up with her.

Upon closer look, her pupils are dilated and she has scratch marks on her face. I hate to think it, but she might be on something.

"Man, I can't believe you're here. I was actually just thinking about you the other day. Remember that party that we went to a couple of months ago? That was fun, right? Well, except for what happened at the end," she continues on without waiting for me to answer any of her questions or ask questions about what happened at the end, which I want to. Really, really badly. "But still, it was pretty fun up until then, right?" I start to nod, but she keeps going. "You got your first kiss that night, didn't you? I almost forgot about that." She scratches at her arms, her jaw twitching. "Please tell me he's kissed you again. If he hasn't, I'm so gonna kick his ass." She pauses for a beat and I almost manage to get the question out about who kissed me that night, but she starts babbling again. "He's a good kisser, right? I bet he is. Not that I'd ever want to kiss him. But a lot of girls do."

"Who's a good kisser?" I sputter while I have a chance.

She looks at me like I'm crazy. "Duh. Kingsley. The only guy you've kissed. Well, unless you've kissed someone else since the party. I'm hoping you haven't, because you two would make an awesome couple. It's part of the reason why I invited you to the party—so he could have a chance to spend time with you. Not that I didn't want to hang out with you. You're so awesome." She laughs, like the conversation is amusing.

Like Kingsley kissing me is something simple.

But it's not.

Even before the accident, it would've been complicated.

But now...

Warm lips on mine...

Breathing air into my lungs...

"I'm scared," I whisper as the water rises toward my head.

"I've got you," someone whispers in my ear. "I promise I won't let anything happen to you, Har."

"Oh my hell," I mutter as it clicks.

Kingsley.

Kingsley saved me that night.

I can see it now, see his face in the midst of the darkness, like a light guiding me back to my life.

But why was he there at all? And why hasn't he told me he was the one who saved me? Why is he letting Foster take the credit?

Is that what he wants to talk to me about tonight?

"Crazy girl, are you okay?" Star waves her hand in front of my face, yanking me from my thoughts. "You look sick." She leans forward, examining me closely. "Wait. Are you on something?" Her eyes widen. "Please say you didn't take something someone here gave you? Didn't Kingsley tell you the rules?"

I'm about to point out that she's high when Kingsley emerges from the crowd. He's looking around, as if searching for someone. When his gaze finds mine, he starts toward me.

My heart rate accelerates, yet somehow seems steady.

Warm lips on mine.

Breathing air into me.

Saving me.

He saved me. Kingsley, the guy everyone sees as darkness, but suddenly all I can see is light surrounding him.

So much light.

It's blinding—

"Hey," he says when he reaches me, sounding a bit breathless.

I feel just as breathless.

He saved me.

He was there.

He's the reason I'm alive.

"Hey, Romeo, we were just talking about you." Star grins at him. Kingsley frowns as he looks at her, but she just rolls her eyes. "Oh, don't look at me like that. We were saying good things. I swear. In fact, I was just telling her how great of a couple you two make."

Kingsley pales, his panicked gaze flicking to me. "I..."

"It's okay," I say, even though I'm not even sure what he's about to say.

His gaze searches mine, question marks filling his eyes.

Warm lips on mine.

Breathing air into my lungs.

Breathing me back to life.

I want to kiss him.

Press my lips against his again.

Only this time I won't come up for air.

"Shit," he abruptly curses, his gaze darting to something behind me.

I blink from the trance I fell into and realize sirens have flooded the air, along with flashing red and blue lights. And people are scattering to their cars and into the trees.

"We need to get you out of here," Kingsley mumbles, his gaze returning to me.

I'm about to point out that he needs to leave too, when he turns to Star.

"Can you take her with you?" he asks. "I need to find Porter."

She nods. "Of course."

He looks at me, his gaze blazing with intensity. "Stay with Star, okay? I'll find Porter then come find you."

"What if you can't find him?" I ask, biting my thumbnail. "Or you end up getting arrested?"

"Wouldn't be the first time," he mumbles, but then hastily shakes his head. "Just go with Star. If I can, I'll meet you on the other side of the trees. If not, ride home with Star, okay?"

I nod, but confusion swirls inside me. Why can't he just come with us? Why does he have to go back?

Before I can ask any questions, though, he jogs off, heading toward the flashing lights.

Star snags a hold of my sleeve. "Come on." She tugs me toward the trees. He'll be okay. He can handle practically anything."

I'm not sure I agree with her, but follow her anyway, rushing into the trees. Panic sets in as darkness encompasses me.

"What's on the other side of these trees?" I hiss as I stumble after Star.

"The lake," she whispers, branches snapping around us.

I don't want to go near the lake, but I'm not sure what else to do. So I keep moving with her, jumping at the sound of every snapping branch, my anxiety growing with each minute that passes by, especially as fog rises from the ground.

"How much further is it?" I ask breathlessly as the fog grows so thick I can barely see.

"I think we're getting close," Star whispers. "I think—"

My foot catches on something and I trip forward, hitting the dirt hard.

"Freakin' hell." I mutter as I kneel up. I touch the heel of my hand to my forehead and wince. "I'm definitely going to have a headache in the morning." Sighing, I start to get to my feet when the abrupt quietness of the forest hits me. "Star?" I call out as I inch forward.

My only response is the crunching of twigs underneath my boots.

My heart beats so loudly the noise fills up my head. "Hello—"

A large, cold, bony hand clamps down on my shoulder —a hand that I'm not sure feels human. A scream fumbles from my lips as I run forward, but fingers snag my shirt and jerk me back.

Lips brush my ear. "Shhh..."

My instincts kick in and I lift my foot, bashing it into their shin. The hand leaves my lips, and I waste no time, sprinting away.

Footsteps follow after me, heavy boots hitting the dirt. While the hand may have felt like it belonged on a dead body, the footsteps sound very real.

My fear spikes as I continue to run while digging out my phone. But tears fill my eyes as I realize I have no service. And I don't know what direction I'm going in.

This is bad.

Really, really bad.

Fear pummels through me as I stumble through the

trees, unsure where the hell I'm going. For all I know I could be headed right back to the party—

"This way." Beth materializes in front of me, wispy fog and pale moonlight swirling around her. "And whatever you do, don't listen to it. It's not like me. It's evil." Then she takes off running.

I hesitate for a split second then chase after her, trying to ignore the sound of a voice chasing just behind me, muttering incoherently. The further we go, the darker it becomes. I start to worry Beth may be leading me in the wrong direction, but then suddenly I'm stumbling from the trees and onto the shore of the lake where at least a dozen other people from the party are standing around.

Skidding to a stop, I lean over and brace my hands onto my knees, struggling to catch my breath. Once I can breathe evenly again, I spin around and scan the trees. All that's there is darkness. Lots and lots of darkness.

But I know I heard a voice. Know I felt something grab me.

Beth said it was evil. What was it, though?

Was it alive?

Was it dead?

Evil.

Dead.

Beth.

Ghost.

Paige.

The lake.

The lake.

The lake.

My eyes zero in on the lake. It was the last place I was normal. And now... Well, now I don't know what I am.

"It's pretty daunting when you think about it, isn't it?" Evalynn, Foster's stalker, steps up beside me.

"What is?" I ask, tearing my gaze off the lake to look at her.

Her jeans and T-shirt are covered in mud, and twigs are poking out from her matted hair, as if she was just running through the trees too.

"That you crashed off that cliff." A smile curls at her lips as she glances at me.

"You heard about that?" I quickly shake my head. "Never mind. I sometimes forget how much this town loves to gossip."

Her mouth morphs into a malicious grin. "I didn't hear about the crash from gossip." She leans toward me, her breath reeking of stale beer. "I heard it from Foster. And you want to know when he told me? Right after he fucked me." She smiles smugly as she slants back, tucking a strand of her hair behind her ear. "It was only a couple of days after the accident. Guess he got over you pretty quickly. Then again, he did say I was the best lay he ever had, so that has to make you the worst, right?"

I used to think she was insane, but now... Who the hell knows with all the lies I've discovered Foster has webbed through our relationship.

Everything could be a lie.

Well, that's not true.

I know the person who kissed me at the party was the person who saved me that night. And according to Star, that person is Kingsley.

Speaking of which, where the hell is Star?

"Actually it wouldn't since Foster and I have never had sex," I tell Evalynn as I glance around for Star. My tone is strangely composed, but inside, irritation waves through me, like violent water. Like water rushing into the cab of a truck.

Water splashes around me violently, rising higher and higher.

"Foster!" I call out as water flows in from the open windows. I can hardly see anything but darkness and water... So much darkness. "Foster, where are you!"

"Yeah, but everyone knows you want to have sex with him," Beth sneers in my face, yanking me from the memory. "You're so pathetic."

Perhaps I used to be, but not anymore.

I will never be that girl again. The one who follows Foster around like a lovesick puppy.

"You think I'm the pathetic one?" I question with a cock of my brow.

"I don't stalk Foster, if that's what you're implying," she scoffs. "He wants me to follow him around. He even told me so."

"Maybe he does. Maybe he doesn't." I shrug, backing away from her to end the conversation so I can go find Star and get a ride home. "But honestly, I don't really care."

"You should!" she calls out as I walk away. "He loves me, you know! He does! And I'll do anything for him!"

Jesus, was I that obsessed with him? I want to say no, but looking back I'm not so certain.

Oh my hell, how could I be that pathetic? How could I let myself get so caught up in someone that I couldn't see the truth?

"You can now, though," Beth says, materializing beside me. "And, if you do the right thing with it, you can change what you've done in the past."

"But what's even the right thing?" I mutter from under my breath.

When she doesn't answer, I glance at her and find that she's staring in the direction of the forest.

"You can save us," she breathes out, fog puffing from her blue lips.

"Save who..." I trail off as I track her gaze.

Standing in the shadows of the trees is a tall figure—an inhumanly tall figure. Just like the figure I saw leaning against a street post a few nights ago

"What is that?" I whisper. Then a shudder ripples through my body. "Is that what grabbed me in the trees?"

"That's what'll keep you from the truth, if you're not careful," Beth whispers. "Because while some of us are good and only want to be saved, there are some that don't want that—who don't want us to be saved. And they'll do anything to keep things that way—to keep the truth buried."

"What truth?" I start to ask, but she vanishes like the thinning fog.

I glance back at the trees and find the abnormally tall figure gone. But I shiver as Beth's warning echoes through my mind.

She never said what the figure was, but I have a feeling it isn't human, which means I'm seeing more than just ghosts. That article I found said people who died and came back to life could sometimes communicate with the dead. I'd assumed it meant ghost. But what if there's more to death than just spirits.

I shiver, inching away from the trees and turn to go

find Star, wanting to get the hell away from this damn lake.

A handful of minutes later, I find her just a ways up the shore, talking to a group of people.

"Fuck, I'm so glad I found you," Star says, rushing toward me. "Kingsley would've kicked my ass if I lost you."

"I'm sure he wouldn't have," I say, but when I really think about it—what he's done for me—I have to wonder if maybe he would. "Where did you go anyway? I swear, it was like one minute you were there in the trees with me and then suddenly you were gone."

She shrugs, wrapping her arms around herself. "I have no idea. One minute you were beside me and then you weren't. I called out to you, but you didn't answer."

My brows dip. "I didn't hear you call out for me."

"Well, I did. Not very loudly, though. I was worried the cops might hear me or something." Her gaze strays to the trees, and I notice her shudder. " It scared the shit out of me when I realized you were gone. This place has always given me the creeps." She blinks a couple of times, and then focuses on me. "But anyway, I got a text from Kingsley a couple of minutes ago. I guess him and Porter are getting hauled into the station, so you're supposed to ride home with me. I'm actually riding home with a couple of friends of mine, but their cool with dropping you off. The driver's sober too—Kingsley triple checked with me about that."

I nod, grateful Kingsley found me a ride home, but something doesn't add up.

"How did Kingsley text you if he's arrested?" I wonder as we hike up the shore toward the dirt road where a few cars are parked.

Headlights shine in the darkness, casting light across the rippling water, and making memories ripple inside me.

Kingsley was in the truck with me the night of the accident, but where was Foster? Did he swim out and leave me in the truck? Or did he somehow get out of the truck before it crashed?

"Hmmm... I'm not sure about that," Star says, but I detect a hint of uneasiness in her tone.

"She's lying," Beth whispers in my ear. "But don't worry, you can trust her... for now."

She leaves it at that, leaving me to wonder what she meant by: *for now?*

That in the future I won't be able to trust Star?

I remain fairly quiet during the drive home, stuck in my own head. It doesn't really matter how quiet I'm being, though. The only person I know in the car is Star and she's busy talking to the driver, a guy with short brown hair and a scar on his cheek. And the two guys riding in the backseat with me reek of vodka and are passed out.

A couple of minutes before we arrive at my house, I receive a text. I expect it to be either my mom or Foster, but it's from Kingsley. I haven't received a message from him in years. The only reason I have his number is because I have all the Avertonson's numbers.

Kingsley: Hey, just wanted to make sure you got home okay.

Me: I'm almost home, but yeah, I'm okay.

I'm worried about you, though. Star says you were arrested?

Kingsley: It's not that big of a deal. They're just holding me for a few hours to ask me some questions about the party. Porter's here too, along with a couple of other people that were at the party.

Me: What questions are they asking you?

Kingsley: About if we knew of any drugs getting passed around... I guess some girl went to the emergency room a little before we showed up at the party. From what I've been told, she was doped up on something that she swears she didn't take on her own—it's why the cops showed up.

Me: Jesus, that happens a lot here, doesn't it?

Kingsley: Yeah, it's becoming a big problem... It's why I was so persistent on you not drinking or smoking anything.

Well, that explains one mystery, but there's still a ton of unanswered questions.

Me: How are you texting me if you're in jail? I thought you only get one phone call or something like that?

Kingsley: Technically I'm not arrested. I'm just here getting questioned. And I know the officer who's questioning us so he's giving me a free pass to text whoever I need to.

The fact that he knows the officer makes me wonder how many times he's been arrested. I know of one time in particular, but like I've said before, I don't know much about Kingsley despite having known him almost my entire life.

Still, I'm not afraid of him, that he's been arrested, that he knows officers.

Safe.

Safe.

Safe.

Kingsley: Hey, I have to go. Text me when you're in your room so I know you made it home safely.

Me: Okay.

I move to put my phone away as the car slows to a stop. When I glance up, I see we're parked across the street from my house. Thankfully, the lights are still off, which means my mom doesn't know I snuck out.

"Thanks for the ride," I say as I push the door open to get out.

Star rotates around in her seat. "Anytime, crazy girl."

She gives me a smile that doesn't quite reach her eyes. "We'll have to hang out sometime again. Preferably without cops around."

I smile, but something feels off. "That sounds fun. I've actually tried to text you a few times over the last couple of months, but I think you got a new number."

"Nah, I lost my phone and didn't have enough money to replace it," she explains. "But I usually borrow one when I need to get a hold of someone. And I can get your number from Kingsley or Porter when I need it."

I feel like she's blowing me off. I want to know why, but Beth's words haunt my mind.

You can trust her, for now.

"Okay." I wave and climb out of the car. Then I shut the door and sneak across the grass to my bedroom window. Once I'm inside my room, I take out my phone and text Kingsley.

Me: I made it home safely.

Kingsley: Good. Stay inside for the rest of the night, okay? It's not safe to be outside by yourself this late.

Me: Well, I was going to take a little witching hour walk, but I guess I can postpone it until another night.

Kingsley: Porter's right. You're a smartass. It's okay, though. I like it.

My heart flutters in my chest as I start to text him back—

Tap. Tap. Tap.

I nearly drop my phone as someone taps on my window. My anxiety doubles when I see Foster peering through the glass. The moonlight casts across him, making his face a shadow and his expression unreadable. But I'm not even sure I could ever really read his him. I just thought I could.

He taps on the window again. "Har, open up." He sounds angry and it's annoying.

Annoying enough that I don't want to open up the window. But I need to do this—need to get this confrontation over with.

Sucking in a deep breath, I step forward and slide open the window.

He's dressed in jeans and a nice jacket, his hair styled, making me question if he was out tonight.

"Where the hell were you tonight?" he hisses, his nostrils flaring. "Because according to Liam, you were at some party with my brother, but I told him there's no way you'd be that stupid."

Anger bites underneath my skin. "Why would it make me stupid if I was with Kingsley?"

He gapes at me. "Because anyone who hangs out with him is stupid. And you used to agree with me."

"Yeah, well, I used to agree with you on everything. It doesn't mean it was right of me to do it."

"What the hell is going on with you? Ever since the accident, you've been acting weird. And I know you've been avoiding me. Don't even try to deny it."

"I wasn't going to," I say, rubbing my hands up and down my arms as a chill spreads across my flesh.

His gaze drops to my hands, and his eyes narrow as they slide back up to my face. "Is that my brother's jacket you're wearing?"

I nod. "He gave it to me to wear because I was cold."

He looks at me with disgust. "How can you do this to me? I thought you loved me. I thought we were together. And now you're telling me you hung out with my brother tonight, doing god knows what. And you're wearing his jacket."

Something snaps inside me, breaks like a shell cracking apart.

"I'm also wearing something else." I loathe that my fingers tremble as I reach into the collar of the jacket and pull out the necklace. "Does it look familiar? It should since it's been in your room for who the hell knows how long."

A shadow briefly flickers across his face, but it dissipates quickly.

"I haven't seen that since the day you lost it in the woods, so if it was in my room, someone put it there." He gives a short pause. "And since there's only one other person that knows you lost it in those woods..." He gives me a pressing look.

My fingers curl into fists, my nails piercing my palms. "Kingsley didn't put it there, if that's what you're getting at. Just like you didn't—"

"Don't," Beth whisper so harshly in my ear I nearly jolt out of my skin. "Don't tell him you know he didn't save you."

I want to ask her why, but I can't—not without looking insane.

"You need to leave," I tell Foster, my tone cracking and revealing my nerves. "I need to get some sleep."

Panic flashes in his eyes. "Har, baby, I'm sorry for whatever I did. Please forgive me." He reaches through the window and takes ahold of my hands. "I'm taking off tomorrow for school, but I don't want to say goodbye like this. I want us to be on the same page."

I try to wiggle my hands from his, but he refuses to let go. "What page?"

"I..." He swallows audibly, appearing nervous, but it could just be a façade. "I want you to be my girlfriend. I mean, I know you already sort of are, but I want to make it official. And I want us to see each other exclusively."

I shake my head. "No."

His eyes fleetingly fill with shocked anger, but again, he swiftly erases the look. "Har—"

My bedroom door swings open and my mom rushes in, flipping on the lights. She takes one look at me and Foster, then at the clothes I'm wearing that clearly aren't my pajamas.

"Where the hell have you been?" she demands with her arms crossed.

"I'm sorry. It's my fault," Foster says before I can answer, plastering on that stupid smile he thinks is so charming. "I wanted to spend time with Har before I leave tomorrow, but she said she couldn't go out anywhere, so I came over here for a bit and we laid under the stars for a while—in the yard of course. We didn't want to wake everyone up in the house so we used the window to get in and out. Clearly, we're not as stealthy as we thought." He winks at me.

I want to poke his winking eye with my finger.

My mom relaxes. "All right, but it's really late, so it's probably time for you to go home, Foster."

"I was getting ready to do just that." He grins at me then at her. "I was just telling my girlfriend goodbye."

"Girlfriend?" Confusion takes over my mom's face, but then her eyes light up. "You guys are finally dating?"

She starts gushing and telling us how wonderful it is. And I'm left wanting to wring Foster's neck.

As I glare at him, all he does is smile at me.

In the shadows of the night, I swear it looks sinister.

TWENTY-FOUR
HARLYNN

A few minutes later, Foster and my mom leave my room, and I'm left to stew in my frustration. Why did he tell my mom we were dating? Does he think he controls everything? I can't believe he blamed the necklace thing on Kingsley.

"Are you really that surprised?" Beth appears beside me on my bed, her cut up legs stretched out in front of her, her back resting against the headboard. I've gotten so used to her appearing now that I barely jump. "I think if you really think about it, you'll be able to see he always sort of just did stuff without you agreeing to it. Or with your consent." An underlying meaning edges into her tone.

"What do you mean by that?" I roll over to my side and push up on my arms, sweeping my hair out of my face. "It feels like you're referring to a specific moment, but I'm not sure which one."

Her sunken in eyes glide from her bare feet to me. "Haven't you wondered why you can't remember much about the night of the accident?"

"The doctors said it was from the trauma of what happened." Not that I was ever one hundred percent certain that was the entire reason since my mind was foggy before the accident.

"But do you really believe that?"

"I don't know... I mean, I've wondered if maybe I was drugged. But I don't know when it would've happened to me other than while I was at the party I was at earlier. But how long does it take for those kinds of drugs to kick in?" When she makes no effort to answer, I sigh and sit up. "You know, this would all be a lot easier if you'd just tell me what happened, instead of making me guess everything."

"I already told you I can't tell you everything." She stares at the wall across from my bed, a portrait of misery. "That I've been silenced."

"But what does that even mean? Silenced by what?"

"What do you think, Harlynn? If you're sitting here, talking to my ghost, what do you think has silenced me?"

An aching agony spreads through my body, and for

once I'm grateful that I don't feel emotions as potently as I used to.

"You're dead, aren't you?" Deep down, I think I've always known she was, though. "If you are, tell me where your body is... I have to let someone know so they can find you. And how did you die? What happened?"

She doesn't answer, simply looking at me. "I have to go now. Find out the truth. It's all up to you."

Panic clutches at my throat. "The truth about what happened the night of the accident? Why is that so important to you?"

She shakes her head from side to side, her crimson-stained hair falling into her eyes. "Not about what happened to just you. You need to find out what happened to the rest of them."

I watch as blood drips from the strands of her hair and splatters across my lavender comforter. "The rest of who?"

She leans forward, placing her skeleton-like hands on the bed between us, right on the splattered drops of blood. "The other dead girls. So many girls have gone missing in this town—bodies that are lost—and it's up to you to find them and free their spirits."

I struggle to process what she's saying, my pulse and mind skyrocketing a million miles a minute. I think of how

Paige's body was found right after I dreamt about her, and how Beth's body is still out there.

"There's more dead girls than just you out there?" I ask.

She slowly nods. "So many more. And they're going to start speaking to you more often, begging for you to find them—to find out the truth of who hurt us so no one else can get hurt again."

"Why me?" I choke out, pressure building in my chest.

How can this be happening? How can only weeks ago my main concern be Foster leaving, and now I'm sitting here with a dead girl discussing how I'm going to save other dead girls.

"Because you've seen death—seen what's on the other side of the veil—that divides the living from the dead. And now you're here and you're cursed with being able to see the dead." She slides closer and blood trickles on top of my hand. "You can see the truth. But be careful who knows that. Be careful of the evil ones. They'll try to keep you from the truth."

"The evil ones, like that thing in the forest?" I ask, but she's already fading away.

Fading away like a ghost.

Like a dead girl rotting in an unmarked grave.

But before she fades away completely, she whispers one last set of haunting words.

"The evil ones are both ghosts and humans. Evil lies everywhere, Harlynn, even in places we never expect."

The room grows chillingly quiet after that as she evaporates, taking her haunting whispers with her. And I'm left trying to figure out how the hell I'm going to solve the deaths of these girls. And how in the hell I'm going to tell my mom that I know Beth is dead without looking like I'm insane. What am I supposed to say? That I can see the dead now because I died for a moment. Yeah, that's going to go over really well. I think she's already questioning my sanity as it is.

Sighing in frustration, I reach for my laptop to do more research on this feather mark I've been branded with, and this gift—or curse, depending on how you want to look at it—of being able to communicate with the dead.

An hour later, I'm nowhere near closer to finding the truth, so I decide to do a search on disappearances in this town. And holy motherships, Beth was right. An abundance of girls have gone missing in this town. Some even date back all the way to the 1960s, which leaves me doubting they could all be related. Although, a lot of them have gone missing at parties, which is odd.

Could they somehow be connected? How, though?

And why have hardly any of the bodies been found? In fact, Paige's is the only one that's been found.

Paige, who I dreamed about.

Could that mean something?

I keep searching for more information, but eventually my eyelids grow heavy. I fight going to sleep for as long as I can, not wanting to go into the darkness again. But ultimately, it wins and I have to succumb to it.

TWENTY-FIVE
HARLYNN

Foster is kissing me. We're in his truck. His lips are on mine and his hands are everywhere. Part of me doesn't want him to touch me anymore, but I can't seem to get the words to leave my lips. Then a bright light shines through the darkness, and suddenly he's gone, yet I can't remember him leaving.

Time is moving funny.

I blink through the confusion, blink against the light as I glance behind the truck. Two figures stand in the light, just shadows. I can hear shouting. Then a loud crash. The truck is moving... forward.

But that can't be right.

Forward is the edge of the cliff—

Splash!

The coldness of the water yanks me from my dizziness.

I'm in the truck alone. Water and darkness are surrounding me. My head hurts—my entire body does.

I cry out in pain, but water splashing in my face suffocates the noise.

I jerk back, realizing I'm sinking.

Sinking into the lake.

I panic, frantically glancing around, trying to find a way out, but water is coming at me from every angle. I can't swim. I'm going to die here.

Then a hand touches my face.

"I've got you," someone whispers in my ear. "I promise I won't let anything happen to you, Har."

I blink the water from my eyes and more shock whips through me.

Kingsley is floating in the water in front of me, his blonde hair soaked and swept back, moonlight trickling across his face.

Moonlight? How is moonlight getting in here?

"H-How d-did you g-get in here?" I chatter as the coldness of the water seeps into my bones.

"I swam from the shore after I saw the truck fall in." His fingers splay across my cheek. "Har, I need you to listen to me. I know you're afraid, but we've got maybe twenty seconds tops before the cab fills up with water, so we need to get out of here now."

"How is it not f-full of w-water y-yet?" I ask through

chattering teeth.

He doesn't answer, instead saying, "We're going to have to swim out of here. I know you're afraid of water, but you're going to have to trust me that it'll be okay."

I shake my head as the water rises higher, yet somehow I'm getting warmer—or just feeling the cold less. "I can't swim, Kingsley."

His other hand finds my cheek, so he's cupping my face. "I know that, so I'm going to swim us out of here. You'll have to trust me, though."

Swim us out of here? Trust Kingsley?

Both sound impossible.

"I know it's scary and that you don't trust me," he says like he can read my mind. "But I pinkie swear I won't let anything happen to you. I'll get us out of here." He hitches his pinkie with mine while keeping his other hand on my face.

I shake my head, tears filling my eyes. The water is to my chin now.

"I don't think I can do it. I can't swim... And I..."

"You can do it," he insists with determination. "You're strong. I know you are. And I need you to do this because I'm not going to leave without you. If you don't go, I don't go."

The water reaches the bottom of my lips then.

I'm running out of time, and while I'm terrified, I'm not about to let him die because of me.

Pressing my lips together, I nod. "Okay, I trust you."

Letting out a loud exhale, he removes his hand from my cheek but only to slide it down to my other hand.

"Take a deep breath," he instructs. "Then go down under the water. And whatever you do, don't let go of my hand."

I nod again and do what he says, holding his gaze as I take a deep inhale then duck my head under the water.

As darkness engulfs me, I clutch onto his hand. He pulls me forward, further into the darkness, but I can see light trickling from somewhere. Then I feel my fingers slip from his, and I start to sink downward.

I try to swim, but I keep sinking...

And sinking...

And sinking—

Fingers lace through mine and pull me upward.

"I promise I won't let anything happen to you..."

My eyes slowly open to sunlight cascading across my face. I blink a few times, the memory of what happened swirling around in my brain like a fog lifting.

Foster had been out of the truck when it went over the cliff. Someone else had been on the cliff with us. I'm not sure how Foster's truck got into the water, but I'm starting to wonder if Foster might know—if he was standing near the back of the truck when it went over. One thing's for certain. Two people definitely were standing behind that truck when it went over the cliff.

I think I need to tell the detective what I can remember now. But I need to talk to Kingsley first and see why he hasn't told me he saved me that night. Although, he may have told me last night if cops hadn't have shown up.

Deciding I'll talk to him first then go tell my mom I need to talk to the detective, I climb out of bed. Then I head to the bathroom to take a quick shower. Once I wash the dirt from last night off my skin, I climb out, dry off, and pull on a pair of cutoffs and a tank top, along with some sandals. I leave my hair down and swept to the side, not bothering to put any makeup on.

Only when I'm about to leave the house do I realize how quiet it is.

Is no one home?

I call out to my parents a few times, but no one answers, so I check my phone for messages.

Mom: Hey honey. Your dad and I are over at the Avertonson's helping load Foster's stuff into the truck. I wanted to let you sleep in since I know you stayed up pretty late with Foster. Come over when you wake up, okay?

I have another text and a voicemail. The voicemail is

from my boss so I listen to that first. He's wondering when I'm planning on returning to work, but adds that there's no rush. Still, I think it might be time to at least get that piece of my old life back, since I need money for college. So I call him back and we make an agreement that I'll return on Thursday.

Next, I move onto the unread message on my phone. It's from Foster. I just about leave it unread, but after what was said between us last night, I need to know what he has to say.

Foster: I don't want to leave with us fighting. I'm taking off later this afternoon, but please come say goodbye to me. And we can make plans for when you're going to visit me.

A frown forms on my lips. It's like he thinks the fight last night was just some mild argument between us and I'll get over it.

"He's delusional," I mutter, stuffing my phone into my pocket without replying to him.

Then I step outside into the sunlight and the warm summer-kissed air. Since it's Saturday, many of my neighbors are outside, working on their yards, cars, or just hanging out. While their presence buzzes through the air, I feel a strange darkness clouding over me. Perhaps because of what I discovered about Foster. I don't know, though, it feels like more than that. As if darkness is chasing my heels. The sensation nearly becomes too much and I damn near turn around and run home. But my feet continue moving forward, wanting to make it to Kingsley, to talk to him, to tell him what I know.

To thank him.

Honestly, I don't think I'll ever be able to thank him enough.

But I'll try to find a way to. Somehow.

I'm racking my brain for ways to do just that when the wound beneath my bandage begins to throb. My head soon follows, my temples pounding.

"Evil is near," the wind whispers in my ear.

A coldness trickles up the back of my neck and the feeling that I'm being watched crawls through me. My muscles ravel into tight knots as I peer around, but nothing appears out of the ordinary. That doesn't keep me from quickening my pace, and I practically jog the rest of the distance to the Avertonson's.

When I reach the fence line of the house, I slow to a stop not only to catch my breath, but to survey the situation in the driveway.

My parents are chatting with Kingsley's parents, and Foster is stacking boxes in the back of his truck with a couple of his friends. I have zero desire to see Foster or his friends, and I'm not too thrilled at the idea of being around my parents while they're with the Avertonsons. I can only imagine what they've talked about this morning. Probably how Foster announced last night that we're dating. As soon as my parents go home, I'm going to have a nice little chat about how untrue that is, but I can't do that while they're here.

There's also one other problem.

If I show up and announce I'm here to see Kingsley, a lot of drama is going to break loose. And I have no desire to deal with that right now. No, I have much bigger issues I need to handle first before I attempt to ease everyone into the fact that I'm Kingsley's friend. Well, if he even wants to be my friend. I'm not certain where we stand other than he saved my life.

Chewing on my bottom lip, I decide not to use the driveway to get into the house and backtrack in the direction I just came from. When I reach the corner of the street, I slip between the fences that divide the backyards of the houses from the forest, and use the narrow, flattened path to head to the Avertonson's. The trees haunt me in the distance as I make my way up the path, the shadows of figures dancing against the breeze and reaching out to me. That unsettling sensation of being watched creeps through me again and I end up running until I reach the back door of the Avertonson's house.

I crack the door open before I walk in, listening to make sure no one has gone inside. The house is silent so I slip inside, hurry up the stairway, and to Kingsley's shut bedroom door. It suddenly dawns on me he might not even be home. He was in jail last night. What if he's still there? Or what if he went over to Porter's afterward? Over the years, Kingsley has started spending more and more time away from home.

But I guess there's only one way to find out if he's here.

Inhaling and exhaling, I lightly knock on his door, aware I'm slightly nervous. Not in a bad way, but in a scary, unfamiliar way.

My nervousness only increases when I hear someone heading up the stairway. In a panicked decision, I slip into Kingsley's room to hide. When I get inside, I find him lying in his bed, still wearing the same clothes he had on last night.

Strands of his blonde hair are askew, his eyelids are shut, and his chest is lifting and falling with each soft breath he takes. Like the few times I've been around him since the accident, calmness pours over me as soon as I lay eyes on him. But underneath the sensation is a mild flutter of excitement that only intensifies as I inch over to his bed.

My heart is an erratic mess in my chest as I stare down at him, craving to touch him, to cup his cheek like he did mine while we were in that lake. Maybe it's wrong—touching him while he's asleep, and after how I treated him—but my fingers drift toward him anyway and brush across his cheek, tracing the lines of his face then his lips.

These lips, they saved me.

They're the reason I'm alive today—

Kingsley's eyelids suddenly flutter open and his gaze collides with mine. Grogginess and confusion mask his expression as he blinks up at me.

"I'm dreaming, right?" he murmurs, his eyes scanning my face. "I have to be..." Then he reaches up, cups the back of my head, and guides my lips to his.

Warm lips on mine...

Breathing air into my lungs...

Breathing life into me...

Kingsley's lips...

My protector...

I kiss him back, letting his tongue slip into my mouth, memories of the last time we kissed twirling around me.

"Har..." He whispers with his eyes shut. Then he kisses me again, sucking on my bottom lip, while pulling my body onto his.

I easily fall onto him and don't even flinch when he flips us over so his body is lined over mine. His hands travel up and down my sides and all I can think is *more, more, more.* Nothing fills my mind but *him, him, him.*

I clutch onto him, my fingernails digging into the back

of his shirt as my legs hitch around his waist. He abruptly tenses and pulls back, his gaze searching mine.

"Wait..." Puzzlement etches across his face. "This isn't a dream, is it?"

I lick my lips. "No."

His expression drops and so does my heart as he pushes off me.

"I'm sorry," he mumbles as he scoots to the edge of the bed and lowers his head into his hands. "I was having this dream... and then when I opened my eyes, you were here and I..." He shakes his head, muttering incoherently underneath his breath.

I scoot to the edge of the bed to sit beside him. "It's okay," I say quietly, but feel a bit stupid.

He thought he was sleeping.

He never really wanted to kiss me.

He lifts his head and frowns at me. "It's not okay. You're... You're Foster's."

I grit my teeth so damn hard my jaw aches. "I'm not Foster's. And I don't want to be... I don't want to be his anything. *Ever.*" I cup my hand around the pendant. "He's a liar and he has to control everything. And... Well, I'm tired of it."

Doubt shadows his eyes. He doesn't fully believe me, which is understandable.

It's time to say what I came over here to say...

"I know for sure he didn't save me that night... That he wasn't even in the truck with me when it went over the cliff," I pause, looking at him. "I also know that you were there."

He tenses.

"I know you saved me Kings—I remember," I continue. "Not all of it, like how you got into the truck. But I remember how you promised you wouldn't let anything happen to me. I also remember how you said if I didn't swim out of there, you'd stay with me... Die with me..." A faltering breath fumbles from my lips as I nervously reach over and hitch my pinkie with his. "I remember your pinkie promise."

He stares down at our interlocked pinkies. "I wanted to tell you... I was going to... But..." He huffs out a breath as he looks up at me, remorse flowing from his eyes. "The reason I was there at the lake that night... no one can know why I was there. If I came forward and said I saved you, the wrong people could find out and..." He doesn't finish, sighing. "Plus, Foster claimed he saved you, and I knew everyone would believe him over me."

"I'm not quite sure I understand everything you're trying to say."

"I know. And I'm being vague on purpose, because I'm not supposed to tell anyone the truth," he says and I frown. "I want to tell you," he adds. "But it's risky."

"It's fine if you don't." Although, I'm unsure if it is.

Beth has been telling me to get to the truth and at the first sign of a hurdle, I'm backing away.

"What if I promised to keep it a secret?" I lift our hitched pinkies up between us. "I'll even pinkie swear it." When he hesitates, I add, "I understand if you don't want to tell me, but I still can't remember a lot of what happened that night, and I'm hoping if you tell me what you know about it, it may spark some recognition."

He contemplates for what feels like forever. "You remember that guy you saw Porter and I talking to last night?"

That was not what I was expecting him to say, but I nod.

"Well, he's an undercover cop that's working with me while I'm an informant—you know what that is right?" he asks and I nod. "Well, Porter's one too. We have been for a couple of months... since we were arrested for... drug possession." He looks away, rubbing his free hand across his face. "Since we'd both been arrested a couple of times before that and we were eighteen, we were probably going to get jail time, but the police struck a deal with us. I can't get into too many of the details, but we've been working to try to find out who's behind the drugs getting dealt in this town, especially the ones being slipped into drinks and laced into joints. On the night of the accident,

I was there at the lake, meeting with the officer in charge of the case to give him an update on some things. We were actually supposed to meet somewhere else, but at the last second I changed the location. And I'm so glad I did because if I hadn't..." He exhales shakily. "But anyway were in my car when Foster's truck went over... And I... I knew you were in there... So I..." He struggles to maintain an even tone, his pinkie trembling in mine. "I swam out there, found you in the truck, and swam you to the shore. But you swallowed too much water and for a moment, I thought..." He smashes his quivering lips together.

My heart thrashes in my chest, my brain crammed with questions.

"You were arrested for drug possession?" I decide to start there.

He raises a shoulder. "I only had a little bit on me, but it was enough to get arrested."

"So you do them? Drugs, I mean." I'm uncertain how I feel about that, that Foster was right about that part of Kingsley.

He gives a hesitant nod. "Yeah. Well, up until recently."

"How long have you done them?"

He fiddles with a hole in the knee of his jeans. "Since I was thirteen."

"Thirteen?" My eyes widen. "That's... that's so young."

He heaves a weighted sigh. "I know. I'm fucked up."

"No, you're not." I give his pinkie a squeeze, trying to reassure him. "Everyone screws up sometimes and you're not doing them now, so..." Unsure what else to say, I offer him a smile.

But he continues to look miserable. "Sometimes I think about doing them again. Things are easier to deal with when I'm high."

My heart aches at his words. "What sort of things?"

He shrugs. "My home life. This fucked up relationship I have with my brother." He gives a short pause. "You."

"*Me?*"

He nods. "I like you, Har. I always have. And as pathetic as this is going to make me sound, you were basically my only friend up until you weren't. And I know we were never close, but it really sucked when you decided to just stop being friends with me without even telling me why."

I swallow hard as his words pierce my flesh.

I'm a terrible person.

I don't deserve him.

And he deserves the truth.

Even though it's difficult through the abundance of

guilt biting inside me, I force myself to look him in the eye. "Do you remember that day on the docks when I fell into the lake? I think we were about twelve years old or so."

He nods confusedly. "Yeah, I remember. When I saw you fall in, I swear my heart stopped beating. And I tried to save you, but Foster wanted to and he started fighting with me about it and... things got so out of hand."

Shock courses through me. "That's what happened?"

"Yeah, and I felt so guilty about it. Here you were basically drowning while we stood by and punched the shit out of each other. It was actually the same day I realized how unhealthy our relationship had become, and I decided I was going to distance myself from him."

I can't believe it. All these years, I'd been so wrong.

I'm a terrible person. And while I've wanted to keep stuff from Kingsley to avoid causing friction between him and Foster, I think he needs to know the truth.

"That day," I say, feeling more ashamed than I have in a long time. "After Foster pulled me out of the water, he said that you started the fight with him and that it seemed like you did it because you were trying to stop him from saving me. He also said that you were obsessed with me in a scary way and that maybe I should be worried about it." I take a deep breath, knowing the next words are going to be hard to say because of the overwhelming guilt I'm feeling. "And I kind of believed him.

Not completely, but enough that I backed away from our friendship." I clutch onto his pinkie. "I'm so, so sorry about that. I'll never be able to forgive myself. And I understand if you can't forgive me, but I'm hoping you can because I'd really like us to be friends." What I'd really like is for us to fuse our lips together again, but I'm not sure if I'm ready to say that aloud. And I highly doubt he's ready to hear it either.

He rubs his lips together, his gaze burrowing into mine. "I'm not sure if that's a good idea."

That remark stings, but I probably deserve it.

"It's not that I don't want to be your friend," he adds. "It's just that, like I said last night, there's a lot of shit in my life right now that I'd rather not bring you into."

"Like informant stuff?"

He nods, wisps of his hair falling into his blue eyes. "That and some other stuff I haven't told you. And after you hear it, I'm not even sure you'll want to be friends with me."

I trace my pinkie along his and he visibly shudders. It makes me want to throw my arms around him and hug him, take away whatever is causing him so much pain and carry it for him like he carried me out of that water. "I really don't think that's true."

"You don't even know what it is."

"So try me." Maybe it's a risky move, but I decide to

add, "Trust me, like I trusted you that night to swim me out of that lake."

He sucks in an inhale and exhales shakily. "Remember that party you went to with Star, and Porter and I gave you guys a ride there?" he asks. When I nod, his throat muscles bob as he swallows hard. "Do you remember when we were playing truth or dare and Star dared you to kiss a stranger in the closet? Someone that you couldn't see and wouldn't know who it is? Well... the guy you kissed... It was me."

So that's what he's worried about telling me? That he kissed me?

My lips part to tell him it's okay, that I know and don't care, but he speaks first.

"And I asked her to do it." He tips his head down, his attention fastened on our intertwined pinkies. "And she did it because she knew I liked you. She knew that I thought you were—that you are gorgeous and smart and funny." He drags his free hand through his hair. "Fuck, I probably do sound like a stalker, don't I? I mean, you tell me you stopped being friends with me because you thought I was too obsessed with you, and then I tell you all of this while we're in my room that has a photo of you on the wall. And while we're being totally honest with each other, I should also probably tell you that I have a few more photos of you in my photography portfolios."

"I know. I saw them." When he glances up at me with a crease between his brows, I explain, "The other day when I was in your room, when I picked up that book and you got all twitchy, I snuck a peek inside it after you left the room and saw some of the photos of me." I sink my teeth into my bottom lip. "I'm sorry for snooping."

"You're fine. I'm sorry for taking photos of you without your permission and coming off as a stalker."

"I don't think you're a stalker. And honestly, while I thought it was a bit weird that you have photos of me, I was never afraid of you because of it. I just wondered—still sort of do—why you took pictures of me."

He gives a half shrug. "I'm into photography and you take beautiful photos. I probably should've told you I was taking the photos, though. But I figured you'd tell me no and I... I don't know..." He sighs as he turns to me, bringing his knee onto the bed. "When I look through the lens, if I see a beautiful moment, I want to capture it as soon as possible because moments tend to fade away and change pretty damn quickly."

I understand his words completely. "Yeah, they really do."

"They really do," he agrees, a brief far away look flashing in his eyes, but it quickly fades away. "But anyway, I'm sorry for taking the photos of you without your permission. And for kissing you that night in the closet."

"You don't need to be sorry for either of that. The photos are really pretty. And as for the kiss... Well, I already figured out it was you that kissed me in the closet. It's how I figured out Foster wasn't the one who gave me mouth-to-mouth—because the feel of the lips didn't match up to his, but the person that kissed me at the party. I still wasn't sure who kissed me until last night at the party when Star let it slip that you were the one who did. And then my mind slowly started filling in the gaps of what happened the night of the accident." I sigh heavily. "Not that I can remember everything."

In fact, there's still so much I can't remember. Like how the truck when over the cliff to begin with and how Kingsley got into that truck so quickly. And how the moonlight somehow shined through the roof of the truck. I also saw light later on.

"It was my first kiss, you know." Why I choose to say those words then, I have no idea. "I mean, the kiss that happened between you and me in the closet."

His gaze never wavers from mine. "I know. Star told me before I kissed you. I think it's also part of the reason she chose me to kiss you, because there were a lot of other guys that wanted to. But she knew I'd be careful with you."

Good god, he needs to stop talking to me this way before I do something stupid and try to kiss him.

"I liked the kiss." *Oh my hell, Harlynn, know when to stop talking.*

He swallows audibly. "Yeah?"

I give an unsteady nod. "Yeah."

His gaze drops to my lips then he leans in toward me. I know there's so many more answers I need, but all I can think about is having his lips against mine and feel that calmness and excitement he instills in me. Feel the safeness pour through me.

Safe.

Safe.

Safe.

Right as his lips reach mine, he pauses with his eyes shut. "I... Are you sure you want me to do this? Because I can—"

I silence him with a brush of my lips and he lets out the most strangled groan I've ever heard, as if he hasn't been touched in years and is both terrified and full of desire.

His hand finds my cheek and like always, his fingers tremble. "I can't believe this is happening... I can't..." He kisses me again, so deeply I swear I can feel it all the way into my soul.

Feel his soul in mine.

Feel his pain.

His need.

His desire.

How much he wants me.

How much he wants to protect me.

How despite how much he wants this, he's afraid.

What the hell is this? Why does it seem like I can almost feel what he's feeling—

A loud bang fills the room and we jerk back, our eyes snapping open.

Two officers barrel into the room and yank Kingsley from the bed, pulling him to his feet. At first I think this is part of the informant thing, but then one of the officers slaps a pair of handcuffs onto Kingsley's wrists.

"Kingsley Avertonson," he says. "You're under arrest for attempted murder."

Kingsley's eyes widen as he stumbles forward with his hands cuffed behind his back. "What the hell? I didn't attempt to murder anyone."

But all the officers do is shove Kingsley out of the room and down the hallway toward the stairs.

I rush after them, my heart hammering in my chest.

No, this can't be right.

I know it can't be.

Can feel it in my bones.

Can feel it in my soul.

In his.

"Stop!" I shout as I rush down the stairway after them. "He didn't do anything!"

No one listens to me, though, and they force Kingsley out the front door.

Just outside, my family and Kingsley's are standing in the driveway, watching the scene in horror. Well, except for Foster. He's standing in the back of his truck, looking at me, his eyes scorching with anger. But I don't give a shit. Let him be pissed off at me. The feeling's fucking mutual.

"Stop!" I run across the grass and toward the curb as the officers put Kingsley into the backseat of the patrol vehicle.

When I get close, though, one of the officers sticks his arm out in front of me.

"Back up, miss," he says as he steers me away from the vehicle.

Away from Kingsley.

Away from my protector.

Safe.

Safe.

Safe.

I can feel the safeness slipping away from me, like my life that night.

I glare at the officer. "You're arresting the wrong guy."

He ignores me, glancing at Janie as she approaches him with her arms folded and her lips set in a thin line.

"You can tell my son not to waste his time calling us," she tells the officer. "We're done bailing him out of messes."

"You have to," I say to her, a rage I can't even begin to comprehend boiling underneath my flesh. "You're his mother."

Her eyes narrow as they skate to me. "Are you defending him? Seriously? You do realize he's being arrested for the attempted murder on you."

"I..." *Words... I can't...* "What?"

She steps toward me, her expression softening as she places a hand on my shoulder. "The accident... A witness came forward and said that Kingsley was the one who crashed into Foster's truck that night. That he..." Her eyes fill with tears. "I can't..." She spins around into her husband's arms.

He smoothes his hand up and down her back, soothing her. "It's okay, hun. We did everything we could with him, but sometimes kids just don't turn out right."

That rage waves over me, all the calmness I felt with Kingsley gone.

Gone.

Gone.

Gone.

"*Come back to me,*" *he whispers as he breathes air into my lungs.*

"*Go back,*" *someone whispers from the darkness—from death.* "*Go back to him. Connect with him.*"

I jerk from the memory, my rage exploding. "Kingsley isn't wrong!" I shout. "And he didn't do this!"

Everyone's eyes widen. Even the officer seems shocked.

"Harlynn," my mother says in shock and my dad's face mirrors her's. "What's gotten into you?"

"That this is complete bullshit," I snap. "I know Kingsley didn't do this. He..." Crap, I promised him I wouldn't say anything. But I can't just let him be arrested. Does he want my help? What the hell am I supposed to do? "And who the heck is this witness that supposedly saw Kingsley's car hit Foster's truck?"

"We don't—" My mom starts to say, but Foster cuts her off.

"It was Evalynn." He jumps out of the back of his truck and hikes across the grass toward me with a smile on his face. But the smile is so faint no one else can probably see it. I can see it, though, like a ghost upon his face. "Apparently her little stalking me habit paid off because she was there on the cliff that night and saw Kingsley crash his car into mine."

"I'd do anything for him," Evalynn said to me last night.

"You're such a fucking liar," I bite out, digging my nails into my palm so deeply blood trickles from my flesh.

Surprise flickers in his eyes, his smile erasing.

"Harlynn," my mom gasps again.

But I ignore her as the police vehicle pulls away, taking Kingsley with it.

I wish I could see him, wish I could tell him everything will be okay. But I don't know that for sure and I don't want to be a liar.

A liar like Foster.

I inch toward Foster and lower my tone, preparing to say *everything* to him.

"Careful, Harlynn." Beth materializes behind him, looking even more boney and broken. "Anything you say to a liar will be twisted into more lies and used against you."

"What does that even mean?" I mutter through clenched teeth.

Foster's brows crease. "Are you okay, Har? Who are you talking to?" He reaches to put his hand on my forehead. "And why do you look so pale? Are you sick?"

"I look pissed," I snap, jerking away from him.

Beth's bare feet don't touch the ground as she floats up

beside me. "It means you need to be careful what you say around him because he'll use it against you. All evil will."

"But I can't let Kingsley..." I trail off as I notice everyone is looking at me like I've lost my mind.

This is exactly what I was worried about and why I haven't told anyone what I've been seeing.

Shaking my head, I storm off, ignoring everyone's shouts of protests.

"Kingsley will be fine," Beth assures me, shuffling after me. "He has you and you know part of the truth. Plus, he has the dead too."

I slam to a halt and slowly turn toward him. "What do you mean he has the dead too?"

She shrugs. "I mean he's like you."

"You mean he can see the dead? I don't... How?"

"He can see them the same way you can."

Slowly and very painfully I realize what she's saying.

"Kingsley died and came back to life?" I say, blood roaring in my eardrums.

She nods. "A few years ago."

"How?" I manage to choke out. "And how did I never hear about it?"

"Because his parents don't want anyone knowing what happened."

I'm almost afraid to ask, but the need to know—to

understand more about Kingsley is greater. "What happened?"

She remains quiet for so long I question if she'll tell me.

But then she whispers in a hollow tone, "He tried to inflict death upon himself."

An agonizing pain stabs through my chest.

Kingsley tried to take his own life.

God, how much pain was he in?

Is he still in that much pain?

I picture the sorrow in his eyes and my stomach lurches. As vomit burns the back of my throat, I sprint down the sidewalk as fast as I can until I reach the front lawn of my house. Then I drop to my knees and empty out the contents of my stomach into the bushes as pain crushes at my chest. But I'm not positive the pain belongs to me.

I can feel him. Kingsley. Inside me, under my flesh, in my veins, in my heart. *Everywhere.*

"Beth," I whisper as I flop back down on the grass, my skin clammy, my chest and stomach sore from the vomiting. "Why do I feel so in tune with Kingsley? Is it because he saved me? Or is it because of something else?"

She kneels down beside me. "It's because of how he saved you."

I close my eyes as the pain inside me blazes. "And how exactly did he save me?"

"By intertwining your souls."

My eyes pop open. "*What?* How... Huh?"

"He doesn't know he did it." She starts to fade away. "You've been cursed with seeing the truth of the dead, which includes Kingsley." Her voice is like the wind. "Use that curse to free him—to free all of us. To find the truth." She dissolves before I get a chance to ask her questions.

It probably doesn't matter, though, since she rarely gives me straightforward answers.

Still, her riddled words echo into my mind until it's all I can hear or think about.

Find the truth.

Find the truth.

Find the truth.

Truth.

Truth.

Truth.

Summoning a deep breath, I get up to do just that. And I won't stop until I free the dead girls. And Kingsley, not just from jail but from his agonizing pain I can feel apparently in our intertwined souls.

TWENTY-SIX
HARLYNN

When I get into my house, I lock myself in my room. Then I send Porter a text so I can talk to him about whether or not I should come forward about Kingsley saving me. Not that I'm thrilled to be asking Porter for help. But it could be worse. I could have to ask Foster.

He doesn't respond, though, so while I wait for my parents to return home, I busy myself with searching online about this curse death has bestowed upon me, and the intertwining souls thing Beth mentioned. When my parents do show up, I know they're going to bang on the door and demand some answers as to why I flipped the hell out.

I wish I could tell them the truth, tell them what's going on with me, and they'd simply understand. But it's not going to be that easy, which I guess is okay. The complications can be my penance for how I treated Kingsley in the past, for the terrible person I was.

Just like I expected, about a half an hour later, someone knocks on my door.

"Harlynn, we need to talk about what happened," my mom says, knocking on my door again.

"I don't want to talk about it right now," I tell her as I scroll through the article I read the other day about the feather-shaped wound.

Since Beth can't give me answers and I haven't been able to find out more online, I'm going to try to get ahold of the person who wrote this article and see if I can ask them some questions. Maybe if I can find out more about what's going on with me, I can get closer to figuring out how I'm supposed to save all these girls. Because as of now, I have no clue where to start.

"Harlynn," my mom warns. "Open the damn door."

"Mom, I just need some space for a bit so I can try to process what just happened."

"I understand that, but the way you acted while you were over at the Avertonson's... Something's going on with you. I think something has been ever since the accident."

I need to tell her something so she'll leave me alone.

"I know," I reply as I click on an *Email the Author* button at the bottom of the page. "And I think I should make an appointment with a therapist, like you suggested the other day."

She briefly pauses. "Okay, that sounds good. Do you want me to do that for you?"

"No, I want—*need* to do it for myself." And while I may not want to go to a therapist, I might have to so my mom can have peace of mind and give me some breathing room.

"Okay... But I still don't understand why you got so upset with Foster. He cares about you—you know that. And this has to be hard on him knowing that his own brother..." Her voice cracks. "I mean, Kingsley has gotten into trouble before, but this..."

Anger simmers under my skin, but I remind myself to remain calm. That she's only reacting this way because of how Kingsley's parents portray him.

"Mom, can you do me a favor?" I ask cautiously.

"Of course."

"Can you please not just assume that Kingsley did this? From the bits and pieces I can remember about the night of the accident... It doesn't seem like it was him. Plus, this Evalynn girl who supposedly witnessed the accident happen isn't a reliable source. Trust me. I knew her in school and she stalked Foster."

"Wait..." She gives a short pause. "Was she the one who ruined Foster's car that one time?"

"Yep."

"Oh dear. I need to call Janie and see if she realizes it's the same girl. But I think you and I should still talk about what happened, but not through a closed door."

Relief washes through me.

I think I may have gotten her to question Kingsley being guilty. At least enough that she's going to talk to Janie.

I line my fingers to the keyboard, contemplating what I should type in the email. "Can you give me a few minutes?"

It takes her a second to answer. "Okay... But I'll be right out in the living room."

Great. At this rate, she's never going give my space.

Sighing, I focus on typing the email.

Hey,

I'm not sure how much you believe in the article you wrote, but I think I may be one of these people that died and came back to life marked with the Sight of Fallen Darkness. I'd really like to know more about it. If you could email me back, that'd be great.

Sincerely,

Dead Girl

I shut my laptop and move to climb off the bed when my phone rings. When I glance at the screen, my heart nearly leaps out of my throat.

"Hey?" I answer with a shaky breath.

"Hey." The sound of Kingsley's voice makes my stomach flutter, and the pain in my chest momentarily dissipates. "I'm glad you answered. I was a bit worried you might not, considering... Well, I'm sure by now you know the full story of why I was arrested."

"I do, but I know you didn't attempt to murder me." I move to my closet to avoid risking my mom overhearing this conversation—I wouldn't put it past her to be right outside my room instead of in the living room. "I was going to speak up and say that you saved me that night, but I'm not sure if you want me to. If you do, I will. In fact, please say you want me to."

"No, don't," he replies in a rush and my heart sinks. "The officer in charge of my informant case is going to handle this. He was with me at the lake, so he can speak for me as a witness that I didn't do this. But he's going to handle it discreetly so my cover doesn't get blown."

Relief pours through me. "Okay. I won't say anything if you don't want me to. But how long will it be until you get out?"

"It shouldn't be too long. Hopefully by the end of the day because I have to be somewhere tonight."

"You mean in the drug world?" I crack a nervous joke.

He chuckles and I feel the pain in my chest momentarily alleviate.

Our souls are intertwined. Is that why I can feel what he's feeling?

"Yeah, pretty much." He gives a brief pause. "But I'm still confused why someone said I did this."

"It was Evalynn. Do you know who she is?"

"Vaguely. She went to our school, right? And had a stalking problem with Foster?"

"Yeah, but I'm not so sure anymore if she was actually a stalker. In fact, I think she might secretly be friends with Foster."

A beat skips by.

"How do you know it was her who said I hit the truck off the cliff?" he asks with a hint of puzzlement in his tone.

"Foster told me, which I think is weird because last night I ran into Evalynn and she made a point to tell me she'd do anything for Foster."

Silence stretches across the line.

"You think Foster told her to say she saw me cause the accident?" he asks in a low tone.

I slide down onto the floor and rest against the wall. "I'm not sure... Either it was just a strange coincidence she said that the night before this happened, or... yeah, I think he may have told her to say it."

More silence and I grow worried my accusations might be crossing a line.

But then he says, "Can you stay away from Foster until I can look into this more?"

"I wasn't planning on going near him, so yeah, I'd be more than happy to. And besides, he's leaving for school today anyway."

"Actually, he's not. I called my mom right before I called you, and during our ten second conversation, she told me Foster was going to stay a few extra weeks to make sure everything's okay with her and my dad. I think it was her way of making a point to remind me that he's the good son. Of course, she made that point pretty fucking clear when she told me I was no longer part of the family and to stay out of contact with them. Then she hung up on me so yeah... I guess that's that."

"Kingsley," I whisper, sadness spreading through my chest.

A sadness that doesn't belong to me.

There's so much I want to say to him and ask him about, mainly about what Beth told me. How he may have tried to inflicted death upon himself. I want to take his pain away and trap it inside me. But I'm not sure where to start or if this is even a discussion we should have over the phone while he's in jail. I want to see him when we speak so he can see my face, see that I speak the truth when I tell him that I'm glad he's here, that he didn't die.

"No, it's okay," he utters before I can say anything else. "It's not anything I haven't heard before."

"Still..." I think about my mom sitting in the living room so she can be close to me and make sure I'm okay, like a good parent would do. Kingsley has never really had that, had someone who cared deeply about him. I know that now—can feel it. "I care about you. And I want you to be part of my life, and I want you to let me be part of yours."

The line grows so quiet I worry he hung up on me.

"You don't need to feel obligated to be nice to me just because I saved you," he finally utters.

Is that what he thinks?

Can I really blame him for thinking that way?

No, not with how I've treated him in the past.

"I don't feel obligated," I swear. "I know I didn't start being nice to you until after you saved me, but that's only because I can see things clearer now. And I can see that you're a good person. A person that I want in my life." *Who I want to kiss. Save. Take away your pain.*

"Okay... If that's what you want." He sounds defeated.

I nervously chew on my thumbnail. "I do, but only if you want it too. I don't want to force you to be my friend."

"Har... I've wanted to be your friend since the day I dug that hole in your backyard and you hugged me after we all got into trouble. No one had ever been that nice to me before and I... I just wish things could've been different between us."

Good god, that's what he considers nice? A simple hug?

"Things can be different now if you want them to be." I hold my breath, waiting for him to respond.

"I want," he whispers. "I really do."

I free a trapped breath I wasn't even aware I was holding.

I can *feel* that he really wants this.

"I want that too," I say.

"Good," he says and I can feel the relief in him. But then he grows tense again. "I have to go. I'll talk to you more when I get out of here. Be safe, okay? Don't go outside at night alone and... stay away from my brother."

"I will," I assure him.

"All right." A tiny drop of doubt resides in him. "I'll talk to you later then."

"Okay."

He hangs up and I do the same with a sigh.

He still acts as though he doesn't fully believe me when I say I'm done with Foster. But I'll prove to him that I am. I'll have nothing to do with Foster. And I'm going to inform everyone that Foster and I aren't dating.

As I walk out of the closet, making all these vows to

myself, my computer pings with an incoming email. I walk over to the bed where my laptop is and see that the author has responded to my message.

I open up the message and read it:

Dear Dead Girl,

If you want to learn more about your gift, I can help you with that. But it's going to take me a few days to set up a location where we can meet safely. I'll be in touch. For now, be careful of the Death Stealers. If you haven't figured out what those are, they're the tainted souls that roam the earth looking for weak souls to feed on. If you see one, don't trust it. They're master manipulators and will try to trick you into doing something that's evil and that benefits them.

Sincerely,

Death

The entire email creeps the hell out of me, but them signing it as Death is beyond creepy.

And what am I supposed to do when they email me back? Just go meet some stranger alone? No, I'm going to have to tell someone and since the only person I trust right now is Kingsley...

Crap, I think I'm going to have to tell him about my curse. But if Beth was right and Kingsley once died and came back to life, maybe he'll understand. In fact, I know he will. I can feel it.

Can feel him inside me.

It makes me wonder how he saved me that night.

Beth said he intertwined our souls, but that he doesn't know he did. What does that mean exactly? Because I couldn't find anything about it on the internet. And at this point, the possibilities seem endless.

"A lot of things are endless, especially death."

I jolt, spinning around. "Beth, why do you..." I trail off as I realize she's not alone.

Paige is standing beside her, only she's not the Paige I remember, but a decaying skeleton of the girl I once knew. Beside her is a girl around my age that I've never seen before, and her hairstyle and torn dress look outdated.

"What is this?" I whisper.

"Your gift is growing stronger," Beth says. "And until you save us, it's going to get stronger and stronger until death is all you see."

"But I don't even know where to begin to figure out how to save you?" I whisper as another dead girl with dark hair materializes behind them.

"You'll figure it out," Beth says, blood dripping down her cheek.

I force down a shaky breath. "And what if I don't?"

"Then the second life you've been given will fade away from you," she replies ominously. "And the person who gave it to you—who tethered his soul to yours—will fade away as well. Fade into the darkness."

Then just as suddenly as the dead girls filled up my room, they fizzle away. And once again, I'm left trying to figure out the full meaning of Beth's words.

What did she mean by my second life, and the person's life that saved me, will fade away into the darkness if I don't save them? That I'll fade away? That Kingsley will fade away?

That we'll both die?

No, I won't let that happen.

I'll make sure I find a way to save those girls.

I'll make sure I save Kingsley.

TWENTY-SEVEN
KINGSLEY

I can't believe Foster might be the reason I'm here at the police station.

No, I retract that statement. I can believe it. It sucks, though, knowing he hates me that much. The sucky part is my parents have started to hate me too. It's not like they loved me that much to begin with, but at least before this happened, they didn't disown me. But I guess it was a long time coming.

It's a good thing I'm used to dealing with this shit.

And dealing with it alone.

I haven't always been as good at dealing with it, though. There was a point in my life, when I was around thirteen, that I stopped wanting to deal with everything. When I tried to stop existing. The pain I constantly carried around, it was becoming unbearable. At least, I believed so at the time. But trying not to exist anymore didn't work and I ended up coming back. I wasn't the same person as I was before. My brief taste of death changed me, made me *feel* things I could barely comprehend. It's why Harlynn's statement of feeling different after she came back from death struck so close to home. I just hope she doesn't struggle with her near-death experience as much as I did—it's part of the reason why I got into drugs. But I don't struggle with it so much anymore. I've gotten used to the difference in me.

Well, I had until a few weeks ago after I saved Harlynn. And it only became worse when Harlynn started talking to me, touching me, letting me kiss her.

Her lips are so soft... She tastes so good... Feels so good...

I blink from the memory as a spark of fear zaps through me.

A fear that doesn't belong to me.

Harlynn is frightened, but why?

I massage my aching chest while glancing around at the empty room I'm being held in. I need to get out of here so I can go see Harlynn and find out what the hell is scaring her. But detective Brandlee said it could take a few hours for my release to be processed. I'm just glad I'm being released. And I'm glad Harlynn didn't believe I actually did what I've been accused of.

I could never do something like that to her or anyone

else, no matter what people think of me. It makes me sick just thinking about her hurting. I've only ever wanted her safe.

Deep down in the lightest parts of my darkened soul, I know I should keep my distance from her, that I'm not right for her, that I'm tainted. But she seems intent on getting close to me. And this thing... this growing connection I've been feeling with her for the last couple days is complicating things. How am I supposed to stay away from her when I can *feel* how much she wants to be around me, and all I can think about is wanting to be around her? But I question if she only wants me because I saved her.

I swallow hard as I recall that haunting night, how I'd been talking to the detective on the shore when I felt a sharp sting of fear pierce through me, and somehow I knew Foster's truck was going to fall off the cliff.

It wasn't the first time I'd felt an omen like that. It had happened a couple of times since I'd died and come back to life. But I'd never felt anything that major or potent. Suddenly, it made sense why earlier that night, I'd unexpectedly got a feeling I needed to change the meeting location with the detective—because I needed to be near the lake.

I'd tried to call Harlynn to warn her, but she wouldn't answer her phone. I even tried calling Foster, but he didn't answer either. So, I jumped out of the car and ran for the shore. The second my feet touched the water, the truck fell off the cliff. I dove into the water and swam. After that, things become a bit blurry and truthfully, I'm not sure how I made it to the truck before it was completely submerged in the water.

Somehow I managed, though, to get there in time, and I swam Harlynn out of that truck and out of the lake. But by the time we made it to the shore, she wasn't breathing, and every single part of me was screaming that she was going to die. But I refused to let that happen.

I tried to give her mouth-to-mouth, tried to pump the life back into her heart with my hands, but nothing I did worked and I became desperate. Desperate enough that I started begging.

I'd done enough research to know there were things living in this world that were connected to the Land of the Dead. That the feather-like mark on my back connected me with these things. And sometimes, out of the corner of my eye or from a distance, I had seen tall figures that didn't appear humanlike and people that looked like they were rotting. But I'd never tried to speak to any of them until that night.

"Let her live," I begged to the night sky. "Take me instead. Take me, please. Just don't let her die. I'll do anything."

As the pleading words poured from my soul, light started twirling around me. Then heat began to sear in my chest, as if something was being ripped from it. Seconds later, Harlynn's eyes opened and she coughed out the water that was filling her lungs.

Whenever I think back to that moment, I swear it was as if some of my life left my body and went into hers. But I doubt that's the case.

Still, I know something mysterious and strange happened between us since I can feel what she's feeling now. The sensation was brief at first, but has been intensifying the more time passes. Part of me wonders if she can feel it too, but so far, she hasn't shown signs of being able to.

I worry, though, that dying and coming back to life changed her like it changed me. Even before the accident, I worried about her, although it was usually from a distance. After she died, that worry spread through me like the blood in my veins.

I worry so much about her. About what she sees. About how different she is now. If there's a feather-shaped mark hidden underneath that bandage on her wrist. If that mark makes her feel and see things like I do—

I'm yanked from my worries as the door swings open and detective Brandlee enters the room.

He's in his forties with dark hair, and he wears a lot of

dark brown suits with god-awful bright ass ties, but he's a decent guy.

"Sorry to keep you waiting," he says as he sets a folder he's carrying onto the table. "I've gotten the charges against you dropped. And the girl that came forward with her allegation against you is being questioned. That way we can make this look more official, but on record, I gave a statement that you were with me the night of the accident and that I saw you swim into the lake to save Harlynn Everly and that you were nowhere near the truck when it went over the cliff. I'm not even sure why this got as far as it did since I reported the incident the night it happened. All I can figure is that the detective working the case isn't aware of our deal. But I'm going to be speaking with her soon to let her know."

"Good. I'm glad." I scratch at my shoulder blade as my feather-shaped scar begins to itch. I hate when it does this. Usually it means something unpleasant is about to happen. "When can I leave?"

He plops down into the seat that's on the other side of the table and loosens his tie. "I can release you as soon as we go over some things." Wariness floods his expression as he opens the folder. "Some information has come to my attention about your brother. Information that could possibly move the case forward."

"Foster?" I ask, even though I only have one brother.

But he's never gotten into trouble before so I'm shocked.

Not that I think he's the good guy everyone believes he is. Foster has a dark side he rarely lets anyone see, except for me. He lets me see it all the time.

When we were younger, it was little things, like lying to get me into trouble, not just with my parents, but with Harlynn as well. He used to do this thing where he'd pull her hair and blame it on me. It was fucking annoying. And at first, I tried to defend myself, but he was such a good liar that everyone always believed him. Eventually, I accepted that I was going to be seen as the bad one.

"Yes, Foster," the detective says, glancing down at the folder. "There's been some claims that he may be selling night kiss. But the source behind these claims wants to remain anonymous, so I need you to look into it. I know that's a lot to ask, since he's your brother, but it could also make things easier."

Shock whips through me.

Night kiss is what we refer to as the drug being slipped into drinks at parties in this town. It's more potent than a rufi and can also be laced into joints. And the risk of an overdose is greater.

No one knows how the drug is being created and who's creating it, but it's what Porter and I are trying to find out. It's why we spend most of our nights hanging out with sketchy people and dealing drugs. It's supposed to help us get a good connection with the drug world, but sometimes I feel guilty about what I'm doing. But then I remind myself that in the long run, I'll have done something good if I help catch the people behind this.

Good.

I can be good for once.

"I can look into it," I tell him. "Just so you know, though, Foster was supposed to leave for school today, but he decided to stay for a few extra weeks because I was arrested. I'm not sure if he'll still stay, though, when he finds out I was released already. Plus, there's another complication. Foster and I... we're not close."

That might be the understatement of the year.

"Hopefully, he won't leave. And if he does try to, we might have to find a reason to keep him here." He leans forward, crossing his arms on top of the table. "This might be the break we need, Kingsley. If your brother is selling the drug, he could know who the supplier is."

I nod in agreement, but my mind and heart races.

If Foster is dealing night kiss, what else has he been doing? And does Harlynn know he's doing it? The two of them are super close. But as soon as the thought crosses my mind, I can feel it's not true.

Feel.

Feel.

Feel.

I can feel so much about her it's almost like she's consuming me.

Not that I care.

But I worry she might not want to consume me.

"I'll start looking around," I tell him. "And see what I can find out."

"Good," he says, closing the file.

We shake hands then he leaves the room to go finish filling out the paperwork for my release.

As soon as he walks out, I dial Harlynn's number.

Even though I'm technically not supposed to talk about the case with anyone besides Porter and the detectives working on the case, I need to tell her what I just found out about Foster. I have to tell her so she'll stay away from him until I can figure out what sort of mess he's gotten into. I just hope she doesn't think I'm lying. A few weeks ago, she might have. Now, she might believe me.

"Hey, you called me again," she answers the phone, sounding as breathless as she did the last time I called her.

I'd wonder what she was doing except I can *feel* she's excited I'm calling her.

"I need to tell you something," I say as I slump back in the chair. "It's about something I just learned about Foster. It's about the case too, so I need you to promise you won't tell anyone what I'm about to tell you."

"I promise I won't." Worry creeps into her voice. "But is it bad? I'm guessing so by the... sound of your voice."

"It might be." I take a preparing breath. "I found out he might be dealing night kiss—that's the drug that's been getting slipped into drinks at parties. The detective wants me to look into it, which means I'm going to have to be around Foster." I pause, waiting for her to say something, but when she doesn't, I grow worried she doesn't believe me. Still, I continue, needing her to understand the severity of the situation. "But anyway, I wanted to tell you so that you'll keep your distance from him while I look into it. I also wanted to see if maybe you knew something about it since you guys have spent a lot of time with each other."

Silence stretches between us, and I can't feel what she's feeling in that moment.

Did she hang up on me?

I'm about to ask when she says, "I might know something about it."

Shock whips through me. I didn't expect her to say that.

"I haven't seen him deal drugs or anything like that," she quietly adds. "But the night of the accident... I was feeling dizzy even before the truck crashed into the lake. In fact, I can't even remember much of what happened after

Foster and I arrived at the cliff other than we were... kissing. After that, all I have are faint memories of me wanting to stop the kiss, but I couldn't." Her voice drops to a shaky whisper. "I can't even remember how far we went. All I know is that I was in the truck kissing him, then suddenly I was in the truck alone. Then I saw a light shining from behind the truck and two figures were standing there. I'm not sure who they were and I have no idea how the truck went off that cliff. All I know is I heard a loud crash and then suddenly I was in the water and you were there and..." She sucks in a tremulous breath. "I've thought about the possibility that maybe I was drugged that night, but it was over an hour after Foster and I left the party before I started feeling dizzy and hazy, and I'm not sure how much time it takes for this night kiss stuff to kick in."

My heart is pounding so forcefully in my chest I swear it's trying to escape. The sensation is partly from my anger toward what happened to her, and partly from Harlynn's fear pouring through me.

"The amount of time it takes for the drug to kick in depends on the dosage you were given." I suck in a breath in an attempt to steady my uneven voice. "When you were at this party, did Foster pour you a drink?"

"No. I poured my own." She pauses. "Although, this guy Grey... I'm not sure if you know who he is, but anyway, he was trying to talk me into letting him get me a drink. I refused, though."

"Yeah, I know who Grey is," I tell her. "He's actually been suspected of drugging drinks, but no one has pressed charges against him. But he's one of the people we're looking into."

"I want to say I'm surprised, but I'm not." She grows quiet again. "But what about Foster? Because if he is dealing this night kiss and I was with him that night..." She trails off, her ravenous breathing filling up the line.

Her fear.

It's so potent.

So is my rage.

What happened the night of the accident? Did someone drug her? If so, I'm going to make them pay.

"I'm going to figure this out," I promise her. "And I think you should tell your mom what you just told me."

"But I'm not even sure I was drugged."

"Still, I think you should tell her. It's important."

She sighs heavily. "Okay, I will, but she's already paranoid as it is so I'm probably never going to be able to leave the house alone again."

"That might be good—it'll keep you safer."

"I'd be safe with you," she whispers through a sigh. "When will I be able to see you?"

She wants to see me? The concept is so difficult to grasp.

"I'm not sure," I tell her. "I have somewhere I need to be tonight, and then I need to start trying to look into what Foster's been up to. Plus, I doubt your parents are going to let you see me."

"Actually, they might," she says, surprising me. "I told my mom how Evalynn was Foster's stalker and that she might not be a trustworthy witness, and she immediately started questioning if you were guilty. She even called your mom to tell her about it."

While I appreciate Harlynn sticking up for me, I doubt this is going to make it so her parents will allow me to see her.

"Thanks for doing that. And I want to see you—I really do. But it might be better if we weren't at your house when we meet up."

"Where are you even staying?"

"At Porter's for now," I say. "But we're going to be moving into an apartment in about a week or so."

"I'd really rather not wait a week to see you," she says and this shaky, excited feeling quivers through my body.

"I'll figure something out. I promise." I glance up as the detective opens the door and motions for me to come on. "They're releasing me now so I have to go. But I'll call you tomorrow, okay?"

"Pinkie promise?" she asks.

A smile tugs at my lips. "I pinkie promise and then some."

Relief trickles through her. "Okay."

We hang up and I spend the next few minutes talking to the detective about the case. Then I'm released and I head out to the parking lot where Porter is waiting for me. But as I exit the station, the strangest fading sensation flickers through me. For a brief moment, I feel as though the world fades away from me.

As if I fade away.

When I blink, though, everything snaps back into place.

Still, I can't shake the feeling that something briefly slipped away from me. But I shove the though aside and focus on the most important problem in front of me.

Finding out if Foster did something to Harlynn the night of the accident.

And if he did, I'm going to make him pay.

ABOUT THE AUTHOR

Jessica Sorensen is a *New York Times* and *USA Today* bestselling author who lives in the snowy mountains of Wyoming. When she's not writing, she spends her time reading and hanging out with her family.

ALSO BY JESSICA SORENSEN

The Curse of Hallows Hill:

Breathing Lies

Whispered Darkness

Untitled (coming soon)

The Rules of Willow & Beck:

Rules of Willow & Beck

Untitled (coming soon)

The Heartbreaker Society Series:

The Opposite of Ordinary

The Honeyton Mysteries:

Chasing Hadley

The Falling of Hadley

Holding onto Hadley

Holding onto Us (coming soon)

The Unexpected Series:

The Unexpected Complications of Revenge

Untitled (coming soon)

The Alexis Files:

Sweet Little Lies

Untitled (coming soon)

The Sunnyvale Mysteries:

The Year I Became Isabella Anders

The Year of Falling in Love

The Year of Second Chances

The Year of Us (coming soon)

The Confessions of Luna:

The Confessions of Luna & Grey

Untitled (coming soon)

The Illusions Series:

The Illusion of Annabella

The Mysteries of Star Grove: Ella & Micha

Heat

Untitled (coming soon)

Lexi Ashford Series:

The Diary of Lexi Ashford

The Diary of Lexi Ashford: The Agreement

Untitled (coming soon)

The Unraveling Series:

Unraveling You

Raveling You

Awakening You

Inspiring You

Every Single Breath

Every Single Kiss (coming soon)

Undoing You (coming soon)

A Pact Between the Forgotten:

The Art of Being Friends

The Rules of Being Friends

The Art of Kissing (coming soon)

Shadow Cove Series:

What Lies in the Darkness

What Lies in the Dark

What Hides in the Darkness (coming soon)

The Coincidence Series:

The Coincidence of Callie and Kayden

The Redemption of Callie and Kayden

The Destiny of Violet and Luke

The Truth of Violet and Luke

The Promise of Violet and Luke

The Evermore of Callie and Kayden

Seth & Greyson

The Evermore of Callie & Kayden

Untitled (coming soon)

The Secret Series:

The Prelude of Ella and Micha

The Secret of Ella and Micha

The Forever of Ella and Micha

The Temptation of Lila and Ethan

The Ever After of Ella and Micha

Lila and Ethan: Forever and Always

Ella and Micha: Infinitely and Always

The Infinitely of Ella & Micha

Untitled (coming soon)

Breaking Nova Series:

Breaking Nova

Saving Quinton

Delilah: The Making of Red

Nova and Quinton: No Regrets

Tristan: Finding Hope

Wreck Me

Ruin me

Untitled (coming soon)

Unbeautiful Series:

Unbeautiful

Untamed

Untitled (coming)

Tangled Realms:

Forever Violet

Untitled (coming soon)

Mystic Willow Bay Vampires:

Undead Secrets & Magical Bites

The Secret Life of a Vampire (coming soon)

Mystic Willow Bay Vampires

Tempting Raven

Enchanting Raven

Alluring Raven

Untitled (coming soon)

Mystic Willow Bay Mysteries Series:

The Secret Life of a Witch

Broken Magic

Stolen Kisses

One Wild, Crazy, Zombie Night

Magical Whispers & the Undead

Untitled (coming soon)

Enchanted Chaos Series:

Enchanted Chaos

Shimmering Chaos

Iridescent Chaos

Untitled (coming soon)

Capturing Magic:

Chasing Wishes

Chasing Magic

Chasing Promises

Chasing Secrets

Untitled (coming soon)

My Cursed Superhero Life:

Grim

Untitled (coming soon)

Guardian Academy Series:

Entranced

Entangled

Enchanted

Entice

Charmed

Untitled (coming soon)

Monster Academy for the Magical:

Monster Academy for the Magical

Monster Academy for the Magical: Hidden Magic

Monster Academy for the Magical: The Monster Trial

Untitled (coming soon)

The Shattered Promises Series:

Shattered Promises

Fractured Souls

Unbroken

Broken Visions

Scattered Ashes

The Fallen Star Series:

The Fallen Star

The Underworld

The Vision

The Promise

The Lost Soul

The Evanescence

The Mist of Stars (untitled)

The Darkness Falls Series:

Darkness Falls

Darkness Breaks

Darkness Fades

The Death Collectors Series (NA and YA):

Ember X and Ember

Cinder X and Cinder

Spark X and Spark

Standalones:

The Forgotten Girl

CPSIA information can be obtained
at www.ICGtesting.com
Printed in the USA
LVHW042236290622
722419LV00001B/128